Eyes on Her

Praise for Eden Darry

Quiet Village

"*Quiet Village* by Eden Darry is a creepy, small town horror with a supernatural element, and I loved every word…The chemistry between Collie and Emily was hot, the reason for them not being together was believable, and I loved the back and forth pull and the realistic little omissions of truth between them…If you love monster horror, being scared, lesbians in a creepy village, then this is the perfect book for you."—*Lesbian Review*

"Scary as hell, and I am not a lover of horror, the paranormal or anything, but in a way I do enjoy it and this was no exception. Eden has delivered a perfect scare with *Quiet Village*, and honestly I wasn't sure I could be any more scared than I was when I read *The House*, but Eden succeed in terrifying me to the point I couldn't put the book down. I wanted to finish it but I loved the sensations and thrill of being scared by this story."—*LESBIreviewed*

Z-Town

"The premise of the story is brilliant…The characters are well-developed and the good guys, at least, are easy to connect with. The bad guys (and there are more than one) are also well done… This is a wonderfully horrific, campy, gory, and romantic tale that I thoroughly enjoyed reading."—*Rainbow Reflections*

"Darry has a fantastic knack for spinning tales. The world building, character motivations and clear writing style kept me excited to read this book."—*Lesbian Review*

The House

"Eden Darry is on my to-watch list. I am eagerly anticipating her new release because I adored this one so much. The pacing was excellent; combining the thriller stalker with the haunted house was a stroke of genius causing threats from both sides and really putting the pressure on…If you have loved *The Shining*, *The Haunting of*

Hill House (TV show), or *The Amityville Horror* then you should absolutely get this book. Eden Darry wrote a wonderful horror. It was exciting, captivating and had me on the edge of my seat with anticipation."—*Lesbian Review*

"For a debut novel, Eden Darry did really well. This book had everything a modern-day horror novel needed. A modern couple, a haunted house, and a talented author to combine the two. The atmosphere was eerie and the plot held a lot of suspense. The couple went between love and hate, and if only they had talked to one another! And the reader just kept turning those pages."—*Kat Loves Books*

"This is why I hate old houses! This was an extremely good debut novel, and it creeped the hell out of me, yet I felt compelled to read on and couldn't put it down. There were many elements that built up the horror of this whole story, but it was such a thriller. The way the suspense was built up and Eden used the other characters, to build the tension was so clever."—*LESBIreviewed*

"A solid debut that is creepy and intense."—*Lez Review Books*

Vanished

"*Vanished* by Eden Darry is a postapocalyptic horror that I thoroughly enjoyed. If you love stories where people have to survive against huge odds, postapocalyptic, end of the world kind of stories, then this is a must-read. If you love stories where something bad is lurking in the background being just sinister enough to make your skin crawl, then this is an awesome read."—*Lesbian Review*

"I really do like Darry's writing—she creates a great ominous atmosphere in her narrative. The initial chapters with the storm perfectly set the stage for what is to come. There's also a suitably unnerving and creepy feel as Loveday begins to realize that there is no one else in the village and a nice bit of tension while she and Ellery are searching houses."—*C-Spot Reviews*

By the Author

The House

Vanished

Z-Town

Quiet Village

Eyes on Her

Visit us at www.boldstrokesbooks.com

Eyes on Her

by

Eden Darry

2024

EYES ON HER

ISBN 13: 978-1-63679-214-9

This Trade Paperback Original Is Published By
Bold Strokes Books, Inc.
P.O. Box 249
Valley Falls, NY 12185

First Edition: January 2024

Credits
Editor: Ruth Sternglantz
Production Design: Stacia Seaman
Cover Design by Tammy Seidick

For my wife and 4AA

CHAPTER ONE

Cally Pope murdered her wife. She turned this apparent truth over in her mind as she ran, poking at it like a sore spot in her mouth.

She burst out of the trees and back onto the path, her feet beating a steady *thump, thump* on the hard packed dirt, *she murdered her wife* ticking like a metronome in her head, feet keeping steady time. She, *thump*, killed, *thump*, her *wife*.

Cally stopped suddenly, a fierce stitch flaying open her side. She bent double and dragged the cold morning air into her lungs. The ground beneath her doubled for a moment, became two paths, then swam out of focus, came back. Her skin prickled hot and cold. Now her lungs itched, and she wanted to reach inside her body and scratch them until there was blood under her nails.

When she knew she wasn't going to pass out, Cally stood up, bent her back, felt it crack, and almost enjoyed the way her head buzzed and her ears roared with the whoosh of blood. She checked her watch: 0715. Still time. Only halfway done, though she wouldn't last much longer at this pace. Cally took a quick drink from the bottle she had clipped to her running shorts, hooked it back on, then took off along the path that led down to the lake.

Her legs wobbled for a moment, muscles wanting to betray her and bring her down low. She fought against collapse, picked up the familiar rhythm, forced her feet to pound the earth again.

Down at the lake she finally stopped. This was the place. This was where her ticking mind finally stopped. Sweat ran down her body and cooled instantly as the freezing morning air touched it. A cold wind was blowing off the lake. Cally watched the kayaker out in the middle, their paddle beating a familiar rhythm on the water. She, *thump*, killed, *thump*, her *wife*.

Cally sighed and finished the water in her bottle. Her legs spasmed and almost buckled and she went to the bench and sat down before she ended up face down in the dirt, and wouldn't *that* be ironic. Stupid. She still had another five miles to go to get home.

Cally leaned back on the bench and followed the steady progress of the kayaker as they made their way back around the lake.

She wondered why today, of all mornings, she was back on the *murdered your wife* jag. Cally had never been tried in any court of law for it, but the Great British Public had judged her all the same and found her guilty. The truth didn't matter, just the will of the tabloids with their lurid headlines, their brand of truth screaming out bile made of thick black ink and puking it onto the pages for everyone to slurp up.

The nation's sweetheart was dead, and Cally Pope had killed her.

Cally sighed. It didn't matter. Some stupid story in an idiotic online gossip rag printed on cheap paper and posted through her letterbox yesterday morning, big *redirect* label on the envelope. The postage mark was stamped in London just like always. Cally knew who had done it—well, not exactly *who*, but someone who must, at this point, qualify as a pen pal if nothing else. The same person who sent the letters. Religiously. They could always be relied on to remind Cally about what happened, about what she did, whether Cally wanted to remember or not. It had been going on for a while now.

Nine months. Time enough to have a baby or have your whole life pulled out from under you in some crappy game of fate. People she was convinced would stand by her disappeared like wisps of smoke. Cally sold everything and left London. More grist for the mill. An absolute sign of her guilt—if any more was even needed. She'd fled abroad—trying to avoid arrest no doubt, the papers said. Cally went to Greece, for fuck's sake. And when the arrest never came, it didn't matter. She'd been guilty for six months by then, and public interest had started to wane just like Nathan—her solicitor—promised it would.

The nation had turned their judging eyes to another poor fucker, and Cally skulked home. Quietly—like any guilty person should—at night on the last flight, and she'd come here to Halesbrook to try to start again. She'd gone back to her maiden name. Not that it would be hard to tie her to the late, great Jules Kay. Not for anyone who still gave a shit about the evil bitch who'd got away with murdering pillar of the community and champion of the disenfranchised, the one, the only, Saint Jules of—

"Fuck," Cally said out loud as the heavens opened with a crack of thunder, and the rain poured. A fierce wind whipped itself into a frenzy and made the trees around her groan and creak. She glanced across the water at the kayaker, who was now struggling to make their way over to the bank of the lake where Cally was. The rain was really coming down, and Cally was soaked through. The rain washed the sweat away but in its place left a maddening itch, one that began at her lungs and radiated out, up and down her legs and across her chest.

Cally stood, meaning to run home. But when she looked across at the kayaker, she could see they were struggling in the rain. The kayak rolled dangerously to the left, and Cally watched the woman—she could see it was a woman now—flail her arms out. A gust of wind caught her paddle and sent it tumbling into the water.

Cally walked out to the shore. The water in the lake looked like someone had reached in with a giant whisk and given it a stir. Of course it was the wind, which seemed to be getting stronger. Water bounced off the kayak, rolling it like a toy in the waves the wind created. The kayaker was in trouble, no doubt about it. She started to wriggle out of her seat. Without her paddle, she probably decided she'd have to swim for it. Bad idea.

Cally stepped into the water and gasped as its icy fingers lapped at her ankles. She called out to the kayaker, but her voice was carried away in the roar of the rain. Cally walked in further, up to her thighs. Her poor abused muscles cried out. She waved her arms, hoping to catch the kayaker's attention. The kayaker was still struggling to climb out when the boat rolled again and nearly capsized. It was still too far from the shore for Cally, a county swimming champion in a previous life, to reach it without swimming out, and looking at how rough the water was, Cally wasn't sure she'd make it.

Just then, the kayak rolled all the way over, its shiny bottom facing the sky ominously. Cally waited for the kayaker to right it. She waited. And waited. The shiny bottom rocked restlessly. Cally waded further out, the water up to her chest, and she could feel the current pulling at her, tugging gently as if to say *come on in, the water's fine*. Cally knew better. But still, that boat bottom bobbed. The kayaker wasn't coming up on her own.

Cally sighed. She started to swim. She pumped her legs as the current tried to drag her sideways and the wind battered her back. If she could make it to the kayak, maybe she could pull the woman out. She was confident she could get her back to shore if the woman didn't fight her, and it was possible she would and drown them both in the process. Cally sighed. She couldn't just leave her out there.

The rain continued to beat down on her head and fill her mouth. Her muscles ached and stung and screamed. She kept swimming. After what felt like an age but was only a minute at most, she came to the kayak. Just as she reached out to touch the boat, she felt the water clutch her waist like a possessive lover and pull her under and away.

She opened her eyes and could barely see anything. The water was murky brown, and God knew what detritus floated past her. She could make out the kayak ahead of her, and inside it, the kayaker. Cally reached out, kicked her legs as hard as she could, and at last felt the water release her. She surged forward and up and broke the surface of the lake. Her lungs screamed out as she dragged air into them. Cally surged forward once more and felt the cold slippery solidity of the kayak. She found purchase on its edge, got her shoulders under it, and tried to push the kayak over.

It rolled once, twice, then crashed back down, shiny side still up. Cally felt her strength draining. She had maybe one more go in her. She went below the surface of the water, pushed her arms straight up, and heaved. She pistoned her legs and shoved with everything left in her, firing herself out of the water. The boat flipped back over, rolled to the left dangerously, then—praise be to God—righted itself. The kayaker flopped inside the boat like a rag doll.

Cally wasted no time. She swam to the back of the kayak and pushed it to shore. Now, the rain stopped. The water, maybe on seeing it had lost this battle, lay back down and went to sleep. Sunshine leaked from behind the clouds as Cally forced the kayak forward. The kayaker coughed once, groaned, then was silent.

The boat scraped on the pebble shore, and the kayaker flopped uselessly in her seat. When she was sure the kayak wouldn't slide back into the water, Cally used the very last of her strength and dragged the woman out of the boat. Cally loosened her life vest—fat lot of good that had done her—and felt the pulse in her neck. Thready but there. She tried to remember anything she knew about CPR, came up blank, and rolled the woman on her side, sure she'd seen that once somewhere.

Cally slapped the woman's back, at a loss for anything else to do. That seemed to do it, though, because the woman gasped, coughed, then spewed brown lake water all over the shore. Cally fell backwards, her legs finally giving out. She watched with relief as the woman puked again, then struggled onto all fours. The woman's breathing was ragged. Cally wanted to speak to her but couldn't find any words. Now it was all over, Cally was shaking and shivering and couldn't stop. She *just* couldn't *stop*. And now that familiar dirge filled her head—*Killed... Your... Wife*—in time with the woman's breathing.

Cally closed her eyes. When she opened them again, the woman was staring at her. A lock of brown hair half covered her face, but Cally could see how pale she was. She wondered if she looked the same.

"Are you okay?" the woman asked.

Cally thought that was a strange question. After all, Cally had swum out into the lake because *she* was drowning. Hadn't she? Wasn't that what happened?

"Your teeth," The woman said. "Chattering. And your lips. They're blue." The woman staggered to her feet and searched in the kayak for something. She pulled out a coat, a thick winter coat, and Cally realised now she was freezing. The cold had settled in her bones and taken hold, and Cally wondered if she'd ever be warm again.

Then the woman was draping the coat around Cally's shoulders, pulling it tight. She sat down next to Cally, and Cally saw she had something else in her hand. A phone. She had a mobile phone.

Cally leaned against the woman and closed her eyes. She listened as she made a call to someone, asked them to come right away. Cally opened her eyes, and the woman was looking at her expectantly.

"What?" Cally asked and sat up straight.

"Do you need an ambulance? Shall I call them? Or my dad, he could take us to the hospital."

"No, I don't need an ambulance," Cally said. What she wanted was to go home. Go home and get in the shower and drive this terrible cold from her bones.

"You're shaking. You can't stop shaking, and your lips are blue," the woman said.

"You don't look so great yourself," Cally said, and then the funniest thing happened. The world started to spin. She tried to focus on the woman, but her face kept shrinking and shrinking until it was just a pinprick. Just a speck of something floating in the universe, floating in that brown, murky lake that was actually a grave, nearly *her* grave, nearly *their* grave.

Just then, the pinprick that was the woman's face went out, and Cally felt herself falling.

CHAPTER TWO

One year ago

Cally watched Jules pace up and down their living room, which had been painfully fashionable until about ten minutes ago. Now it was a mess of broken ornaments and furniture. The beautiful and expensive flowers Jules bought Cally the day before were stamped and crushed into the Persian rug. The shiny parquet floor squeaked and crunched under her feet as she trod broken glass into the wood Cally had painstakingly sanded and sealed by hand.

The initial rage seemed to have ebbed, but Cally wasn't stupid enough to think she was out of the woods yet. With Jules, the whole thing could whip back up as quickly as it died down. The wrong look or sound or word from Cally in the next few moments could set Jules off all over again.

Cally thought of Jules's moods like storms and graded them the same way. Sometimes it was a bit of grey cloud that dropped lower and got darker until you were sure it was going to pour with rain, and then it lifted as if it'd never been. Other times it was straight into Hurricane Jules, which swept aside anything in its path, including Cally.

Cally wasn't yet sure what this was going to be, but she didn't think it would be too long before she found out. Jules was winding back up again. Cally sat on the uncomfortable cream sofa with her legs drawn up and tried to breathe as quietly as possible, to be as still and as small as possible, and hating herself for it.

Suddenly Jules stopped pacing. She turned to Cally and thrust out the crumpled magazine clutched in her hand.

"I just don't understand what went through your head," Jules said. "What were you thinking?"

Cally opened her mouth to speak, to say *I have no fucking idea what you're talking about*, and then her stomach did that sick, twisting somersault thing as she realised she *did* know what Jules was talking about. That stupid fucking interview. The fluff piece they wanted her to do. "Life with Britain's Biggest Gay Icon" or something equally ridiculous.

"You wanted me to do that interview," Cally said.

Jules rolled her eyes and shook her head. "I know *that*. I didn't expect you to throw me under the fucking bus in it. You were supposed to give them your favourite fucking cake recipe and talk about how you decorated the flat. You made me look like a fucking prick."

Cally watched Jules. By any standard she was beautiful—beautiful, charming and warm. Across the country, she was seen as the kind, funny, accessible lesbian even your gran could get on board with. Except that's not the Jules Cally knew. In private, Jules had become ugly, so bloody ugly—like a troll. In her company, Cally could never relax. Every thought in her head ended with *What would Jules say?* or *Would this make Jules mad?*

Watching her now, pacing about the room like some spoilt, tantruming woman-baby, Cally decided. In that moment, Cally knew it was over. She'd had enough. Just like that. Of course, Cally had daydreamed often about getting away from Jules. She couldn't remember when that started but was ashamed to know it wasn't all that long ago. She should have done it in the very beginning, but she'd been weak and Jules was so…magnetic. Stupid, but there it was. Jules dazzled Cally with trips abroad and fancy dinners and flashy parties.

That got old, though, and all the sorry gifts stopped making up for her shit behaviour a long time ago. Cally had wanted to leave her for a while now. Getting away from Jules would be something else altogether, though. Cally wasn't exactly scared of her but—

Oh, who was she kidding? She was terrified.

"Well? Haven't you got anything to say? Don't I at least get a sorry?" Jules said. "An explanation would be nice, but I know how you hate being held accountable for anything."

Cally stayed quiet. She'd learned by now Jules would pounce on anything she said now and use it to work herself back up.

"That's nice. That's just fucking *lovely.* You aren't even speaking to me now? *You* screw *me* over, but somehow I'm still in the wrong." Jules smiled coldly. "I'm not sure why I expect anything else from you after all this time, you fucking useless bitch."

Cally glanced around the room again, at the destruction Jules had wrought. She was so used to the name calling it hardly stung any more. The small hand-painted vase Jules's niece made, smashed to bits. The photos and the plate from Cally's grandmother, thrown against the wall. It would all get tidied and repaired and replaced, except for the things Cally loved. Jules wouldn't care. She'd broken them on purpose anyway, and Cally cursed herself for putting them out in the first place. She knew what Jules was like. Why had she been so stupid.

"Cally? Earth to Cally. Are you hearing me, you stupid whore?"

Cally looked back at Jules. Those eyes which first drew her in with their kindness and humour were stormy, dark pits now. Cally looked into them and knew things were about to get worse. Much worse.

Jules walked towards her.

CHAPTER THREE

Now

Cally sat up and spluttered. She drew in a deep shuddering breath.

"Oh, thank fuck."

A voice above her. She opened her eyes and saw the face of the woman from the kayak. Cally struggled to sit up.

"Maybe you should stay lying down? I mean, an ambulance is coming, so maybe you should wait for them."

Cally ignored the woman and sat up. She pulled the coat tighter around herself. The world swam, and for a moment she thought she might throw up. She didn't, though, thank God.

"That was quite the experience." The woman moved away from Cally. "Bloody hell."

Cally rubbed her face with her hands and tried to clear her head. What happened? She'd gone in the water and saved the woman, hadn't she? She was sure she had. So why was the woman looking at Cally like she was the one who nearly died?

"Well, I guess that's me and the kayak done. Stupid thing anyway. I don't know what I was thinking. Thanks for, you know, saving my life." The woman laughed nervously and rubbed her mouth with her hand. She shivered. Cally though she looked like shit.

"I should give you your coat back," Cally said, for the first time realising the woman must be freezing.

"No, don't." The woman held up a hand. "Please keep it. It's the least I can do."

Cally nodded. In the distance, she heard a siren wailing.

The woman nodded towards the trees behind Cally. "They're coming. Good."

"That was quick," Cally said.

"The base is close to the town, luckily. How are you feeling? Stupid question, I know, but are you feeling warmer, or like you might faint again?" the woman asked.

"I'm okay. I should ask you how you are. You're the one who nearly drowned."

The woman laughed again without much humour. "Yeah, and I'll never live that down. Just, thank you. I mean, it seems like I should say something more, something *meaningful*. But I can't think of anything, except thank you."

"You don't have to say anything. I'm glad it turned out all right."

"Except you could have died too. Because of me and that stupid kayak." The woman looked at the ground and pushed at the dirt with her finger. "So stupid," she muttered.

The sirens were louder now. Cally stood up. For a moment, the ground shifted under her feet, she staggered, her legs wobbled.

"Whoa, I've got you." The woman was suddenly beside her and holding her up.

"Shit. Why am I in such a state? Why *aren't* you?" Cally asked and held on.

"Oh, I am, don't worry about that. I feel like crap. I guess it wasn't easy dragging a lump like me back to shore. And you got cold. You should sit back down. Here, I'll help you."

Cally kept hold of the woman, who lowered her slowly to the ground. It was frustrating and made her feel weak. She'd saved the woman, so why was it Cally was the one who couldn't even stand. Was she really that weak? That pathetic?

"I…thank you. I mean, I know I already said it, but Jesus, you saved my life." The woman briefly squeezed Cally's shoulder awkwardly then pulled her hand away quickly. Cally didn't say anything.

An ambulance that looked more like an estate car drove into the clearing and parked near the lake. A man jumped out of the vehicle before it fully stopped and jogged towards them, lugging a heavy bag.

"Laurie, you bloody idiot," he said, stopping beside them. "I told you about that kayak. Are you okay?"

Cally watched him look the woman—Laurie—up and down.

"Yeah, yeah, I know. I'm fine. She's not feeling great, though." Laurie pointed at Cally who looked away when his laser-like focus landed on her.

"I'm okay, just a bit wobbly. Nothing a warm bath won't sort out," Cally said.

"Are you joking me? A warm bath? What is wrong with you two? No one's going anywhere except to hospital."

"Oh, get a life, Tom. We're fine," Laurie said.

Tom ignored her and knelt by Cally. He unzipped his bag and pulled out what looked like a clip on a wire attached to a machine in the bag. "Here, give me your finger," he said. Cally obliged.

Next, Tom reached into another bag and pulled out two foil blankets. He chucked one at Laurie and draped the other over Cally's shoulders. "This should help with the cold."

No one spoke. The machine beeped, and a piece of paper rolled out the top. Tom ripped it off and studied the results. "Okay, looks all right. Possibly a bit of hypothermia. Definitely hospital for both of you, though."

Cally saw Laurie roll her eyes. "You haven't even inflicted that little machine on me, so how do you know I need to go?"

Tom looked at her. "Because like you said on the phone, you nearly fucking drowned."

CHAPTER FOUR

By the time Cally got home, it was after seven. The sun had sunk low behind the trees that surrounded her property, and she hadn't gotten around to fixing the security light outside her house.

She paid the cab driver and hurried to her front door. She still wasn't used to the utter and complete darkness in the countryside. She used her phone torch to find her keys and unlock the door.

Inside, the house was freezing, which meant the boiler had gone again. Cally hated to be cold. Her entire marriage, Jules had liked the temperature as low as possible, and Jules always got her way. Which meant Cally spend most of her days freezing. Not any more. Now she could have the heating at a solid twenty-three all day and night if she wanted. Most days, she wanted.

Cally flicked on the hall light and realised she was standing on a letter. She picked it up and saw it had the redirect sticker over her previous address, but part of the handwriting was still visible. Cally's heart sank. Another one. She dropped it on the hall table and went into the kitchen.

She'd bought the property and grounds three months ago. The house was a Victorian/Tudor mishmash with a leaky roof, ancient plumbing and wiring, and windows that rattled when the wind blew. The carpets were mouldy in places, and the wallpaper was peeling and stained, but it was hers. For the first time since she met Jules, she had a place that was hers. She could put out her family treasures and favourite things without worrying someone would smash them up in a rage. If she wanted to leave her dirty socks on the floor or a wet towel on her bed, no one was going to pitch a fit and call her a disgusting slag.

Five Oaks Farm was a tired and worn-out glamping site with seven ramshackle cabins and a patchy, weedy field for tent pitches. Cally loved it the first time she saw it. It was surrounded by the National Forest and had the most incredible views she'd ever seen. Her business manager warned her about the amount of work and money it was going to take to get it up to scratch, but Cally didn't care. She wanted to be consumed by something other than guilt and bitterness over her late wife and all the shit in London. She wanted somewhere remote and quiet and sleepy. The town of Halesbrook and this huge forest were perfect for her.

In the kitchen, Cally frowned at the boiler. The pilot light was on and the pressure was good, so she didn't know why the heating wasn't on. Most likely, the ancient timer in the hall had given up the ghost. Cally hit the manual heating button and waited for the decrepit boiler to clunk and groan to life.

Satisfied when the banging and clanging started, she went into the hall to look at the thermostat. It was a yellowing antique from the early nineties but fairly easy to decipher. Cally saw the dial had been turned all the way down to ten degrees. Something dropped with a thud in her belly and left her mouth dry. That was the temperature Jules had liked it.

The thermostat was above the hall table. She must have knocked it on her way out this morning. But wouldn't she have noticed? What was the alternative? Jules had turned down the heating from beyond the grave? Cally snorted and quickly covered her mouth, which was stupid because she could laugh at whatever she wanted now.

Cally wouldn't put it past Jules to do something like that, control freak that she was. Cally's heating bills would have her rolling in her grave. She snorted again, and this time she didn't cover her mouth. She felt better. The sick, rolling thing in her belly melted away. She was okay. She was *good*. Jules was dead, and Cally had knocked the dial this morning. There was no other explanation. She went upstairs to run a bath.

The bathroom was another story altogether. Cally couldn't wait for the day she could rip out the avocado suite and pull up the carpet. Unfortunately, it was pretty low down on the list of jobs. Before she did anything in the house, the business would need to be prioritised.

Jules had left her well off, and with the sale of their flat and the house Cally bought when they separated, Cally was comfortable. But the money wouldn't last forever, and she couldn't imagine living off Jules's money for the rest of her life. Cally wanted to build something that was hers, something she could be proud of. It would be Jules's money which allowed that to be possible, but the hard work and the vision would be Cally's.

After three years living in a nightmare and a whole load of therapy, Cally was beginning to feel like she'd earned every penny Jules left her. Sometimes, like this morning, Cally was overcome with crippling guilt about Jules's death. But those feelings came and went and were absent for longer and longer these days. Her therapist said there might be a day when they went away for good. Cally wasn't so optimistic, but right now, in her avocado carpeted bathroom, she felt fine.

She sank into the hot bath—Jules always liked a cool bath. She welcomed the numbing, prickling heat and dipped her head below the water and closed her eyes. To Cally's surprise, Laurie's face popped into her head. When she thought about this morning, it didn't seem real. She knew it happened, but it felt like a film she'd seen, rather than she who had dived into the lake and pulled Laurie out of the water. Even if it didn't feel real to her, it felt bloody real to her poor muscles. Her back ached and her arms and legs were still a bit shaky.

After she'd been checked out at the hospital, she'd sneaked out despite Laurie begging her to stay so her family could thank Cally for saving her life.

Cally sat up in the bath and leaned back. Laurie seemed sweet if a bit clueless. But then Jules had *seemed* sweet at first. Most people did, until you got to know them and they turned into the actual psychos they really were. Cally shook her head. Why was she thinking about Laurie in the same context as Jules, anyway? Best not to think about that.

Cally pushed thoughts of Laurie from her mind and reached for the shampoo. As she did, something above her thudded then skittered across the floor. Bloody squirrels. The first week Cally moved in, the sound had scared the hell out her. She'd thought someone was breaking in. She was used to it now and didn't find it quite so creepy any more. She'd sent pest control up there to lay humane traps, but the little buggers had still managed to avoid them somehow. The pest control man told her poison bait was the most effective way to get rid of them, but Cally couldn't bring herself to do that. So, every few days the pest man showed up, shook his head at her, and told her there were no squirrels to relocate and she should really consider killing them instead. Every time, Cally smiled and shook her head. It was her house and they were her annoying little squirrels. Plus, her days of doing what she was told were over.

CHAPTER FIVE

Cally clamped the slice of burnt toast between her teeth, hooked her foot around the front door, and pulled it shut. On the way to her car she nearly dropped the tubes stuffed under her arms into the muddy quagmire that passed for her drive. Another home improvement job low down on the list of expensive things she had to do.

Today of all days she'd overslept and couldn't believe it. The one day she had somewhere to be, and she hadn't plugged her phone in to charge overnight. What an idiot. Thank God she was naturally an early riser and, with a bit of hustle, would still make the meeting on time.

Today was a big day. The local council were voting on her planning application to extend the glamping site. She wanted to build an extra five cabins and put in shower blocks and plumbing and electric for twelve caravan pitches. The feedback she'd had so far was positive, but with local councils, you never knew. Once she had the consent, she could sign contracts with the builders and work could start. If her application was rejected…well, she refused to think about that.

The new Cally was optimistic.

The new Cally had a sunny, positive outlook.

She rolled her eyes at herself. Who was she kidding?

Cally pulled away sharply, and the wheels of her car spun in the swampy driveway and splashed a load of mud over her car. Great. Perfect. Thankfully, the tyres gained purchase and she was away. As she turned onto the main road, she realised she'd forgotten to lock the front door.

No time to go back now. And if by some miracle a burglar

happened to come by, good luck going through the million boxes to find something worth stealing.

Cally pulled into the local council car park and easily found a space. She checked her watch. Ten minutes early. She sighed, relieved, and looked up at the drab, grey building where, inside, the fate of her fledgling business would be decided. She took a deep, steadying breath and tried to centre herself.

The hard knock on her window nearly made her jump out of her skin. She couldn't stop the squeal that forced its way out of her. "What the actual *fuck*." It came out as a wheeze, but Laurie clearly heard it because she stepped back with a sheepish look on her face and held up her hands.

"I'm so sorry."

Cally powered the window down, irritated. "What was that?"

"I didn't mean to scare you. Sorry, I guess I knocked harder than I meant to."

Cally's heartrate was returning to normal and her irritation subsided. "Hang on," she said.

She gathered up the tubes and her oversized handbag and got out of the car. "No, I'm sorry. You just startled me."

"Clearly. I am sorry, though," Laurie said. "Can I help you with those?" Laurie nodded at the stuff in Cally's arms.

"No, thanks, I'm fine." Cally transferred the tubes to one arm and used her car key to lock the car.

Laurie regarded her sceptically. "Sure?"

Cally nodded and headed for the council building. "Sure. How are you, anyway? You seem remarkably perky for someone who almost drowned yesterday," Cally said.

"I'm pretty good. You left the hospital sharpish, though. I didn't get a chance to thank you again for saving my life. How are you feeling?"

"Fine," Cally said. "Good, in fact. Bit nervous about this, though. What are you doing here anyway?"

"Oh, didn't you know? This planning application of yours is big news. Half the village has turned out," Laurie said, and Cally noticed with satisfaction that despite her longer legs, Laurie had to hurry to keep up with her.

"Seriously?" Cally was surprised and not sure if it was a good surprise.

"Oh yeah. We don't get out much." Laurie grinned when Cally glanced back at her.

"Why the interest?" Cally asked.

Laurie shrugged. "Well, it's the most exciting thing to happen around here since John Armitage got drunk on his own potato vodka and did a naked jig down the high street."

Cally laughed. "Really?"

Laurie reached past Cally and opened the door for her. "He really did a naked jig. We were all surprised he had such a sense of rhythm."

Cally rolled her eyes and carried on down the carpet tiled, slightly depressing corridor. She checked the doors they passed for the right room. The email said it was on the ground floor, so it couldn't be far.

"But half the village turned up because we're all pretty invested in the outcome," Laurie continued. "There's a lot of local businesses that suffered when the last owners closed up shop. They're all hoping you get this passed because they're banking on it bringing some money back into the village."

"So you're an interested local business owner too?" Cally asked.

"Me? Oh no." Laurie held open another door to the meeting room, and Cally immediately saw she wasn't joking about half the village turning up. Laurie leaned close to Cally's ear. "I work for the forestry commission, and I'm against you getting planning permission. I'm here to speak against you."

Cally turned to face Laurie, her mouth open in shock. Laurie winked at her. "Good luck. May the best woman win. Thanks again for saving my life." And then she was gone, sliding past several people in the back row to take her seat, and leaving Cally alone, arms full of plans and standing stupidly with her mouth half open and everyone staring at her.

She felt her face flush, and anger rose up hot and strong. How dare Laurie blindside her like that, leave her standing there like a bloody idiot.

Cally looked around again at all the strange faces and quickly got herself together. She cleared her throat, gave Laurie her coldest look—which Laurie just laughed at—and walked with purpose to the front of the room. In front of large window at the back of the room was a long table. It was half full, but clearly more councillors were due to arrive. To the left of them, two short rows of chairs were set up. Cally recognised her architect and five or six local business owners she'd spoken to who were going to speak on her behalf and made her way over to them.

Cally caught a woman sitting a few rows ahead of Laurie. She was staring at Cally in a way that made Cally want to squirm. Cally tried to ignore the woman but could feel her eyes on her back as she took her seat.

Chapter Six

So far, things were going positively. Cally's architect had presented really well and demonstrated the eco-friendly qualities of the cabins. Put that in your smug pipe, Laurie, Cally thought. Four of the local business owners had also talked about what a difference additional tourism would make, and when Cally chanced a look at the councillors, she could see a lot of the things the business owners were saying were hitting the mark with them.

Finally it was Cally's turn to speak. She'd painstakingly planned and rehearsed what she was going to say, but as she stood up her mouth dried up and her throat closed. She couldn't remember a damn word of her speech. She looked around again at the people in the room and felt panic rise up and threaten to overwhelm her. The woman was still staring at her.

Just when she thought she going to make a right tit of herself and mess it all up, she caught Laurie's eye. The perpetual self-satisfied smirk was back, and Cally had an uncharacteristically violent urge to smack it off. Then Laurie winked. The anger came hot and fast. Laurie thought this was funny. She thought it was a game. Cally was furious. Her speech came flooding back to her, and relief washed over her, putting out the fire of her rage.

"I'm Cally Pope," she said and was relieved to hear her voice sounded strong and confident. "Many of you I haven't yet met, but I hope to in the coming weeks and months. I haven't lived here long at all, but I'm hoping to make Halesbrook my home, and I'm excited about the future. You've heard from lots of people about Forest Glamping, but I want you to hear from me too, because it's my dream, and I hope that when I'm finished, you'll feel as confident and positive about it as I do."

The next ten minutes passed in a blur. It was like some kind of out-of-body experience where Cally felt like she was floating somewhere above herself. She watched the confident, eloquent blond woman first get the interest of the room, then hold their attention. She even made them laugh. It was surreal.

Cally had never thought of herself as an outgoing, gregarious person. She'd always left that sort of thing to Jules, who had charm to spare. Cally had always been content to hover on the sidelines and occasionally get some of the reflected glory that being with Jules bought.

But this Cally was charming. She was funny and warm and engaging. She answered questions with assertiveness and good humour, and when she glanced at the local councillors, she could see she'd got them onside too. She would get her planning permission. She looked at Laurie and was pleased to see she was no longer smirking. Instead, Laurie looked…impressed. She tipped her head at Cally as if to say *good job*.

When Cally finished, the room even clapped. She was astonished. She felt on top of the world. This was how it must have felt to be Jules. Cally quickly pushed that thought out of her head. She didn't want old memories clouding this perfect morning.

Once she sat down, the local council quickly went to a vote, and Cally was thrilled when it was a unanimous yes. The room clapped again, and then people were coming up to her and shaking her hand and patting her on the back and congratulating her. The woman who'd been staring at her so intently was gone.

"You should come to the pub tonight, and we can celebrate." Laurie spoke into her ear again and Cally turned to face her, pissed off.

"Celebrate? I thought you were against me. Why on earth would I want to celebrate anything with you?" Cally said.

Laurie feigned hurt, and that just pissed Cally off even more. She acted like it was all some big joke.

"You won fair and square. You had them eating out of the palm of your hand, I didn't stand a chance," Laurie said.

"You didn't even speak in the end. Were you just trying to fuck with my head? Did you even care if I got the planning at all? Or was it some big game to you?"

Laurie wiped the smirk off her face. "No, it wasn't a game. I really was against it. Despite what you said about all the eco stuff, traffic will increase massively. All the extra rubbish in the forest, animals being run over by idiot tourists speeding. But I know when I'm beaten. I could see on their faces they were with you. Didn't see the point of flogging a dead horse, you know?" Laurie shrugged.

Cally wasn't sure what to say. Laurie seemed sincere. "Well, you're mad if you think I'm going for a drink with you."

"I didn't say with me. Look, if you're serious about making Halesbrook your home, you should go to the pub later. The people here today, the ones who spoke for you and came to support you, they'll like it. In a village this small, you need to get on with people. It'll look rude if you don't go."

Now Cally was annoyed again. Who did this woman think she was, telling Cally what she should do? "I don't remember asking you for any advice on social etiquette."

Laurie rolled her eyes. "No, you didn't, but you need it. You're like a hermit up there in your big shack of a house. Everyone's curious about you. You finally made a good impression today, and you should capitalise on it."

"My house is *not* a shack. You are so arrogant," Cally hissed. "Who do you think you are? I should have let you drown yesterday." Laurie laughed, and that annoyed Cally even more. "Stop *laughing* at me."

That made Laurie laugh again.

"You're pathetic," Cally said. Before she could say any more, another well-wisher put their arm around her and congratulated her. When she turned back around, she saw Laurie walking out the door. "Arsehole," she muttered under her breath.

The most infuriating thing about Laurie was that she'd been right. If Cally was serious about making a life for herself here and running a successful business, she would need to be on good terms with the locals and with other business owners. She just didn't need that bloody idiot Laurie Flannigan telling her.

Cally sighed. She would go to the pub tonight. If Laurie was there, God help her if she tried to speak to Cally again.

Chapter Seven

As soon as Cally opened the door to the pub, she was hit with a wall of noise. Outside, the tiny high street was dead. Cally realised it was because everyone was in here. The Colliers Arms looked exactly like you'd expect an English country pub to look—small, dingy, and dark inside with old, threadbare carpets and the underlying scent of stale beer and wet dog. But it did have a big open fireplace with a real fire, and it was warm and cosy. Cally remembered going to places just like this with her dad when she was a child.

She immediately recognised most of the people from the meeting earlier, and all of them offered to buy her a drink. She almost said no and then—to her annoyance—remembered what Laurie said about making a good impression. She accepted a gin and tonic, then quickly changed it to a vodka tonic, from the local butcher, who starting talking to her about supplying breakfast and barbecue baskets to her guests as soon as she'd taken her first sip.

She nodded politely and savoured the bitterness of the tonic that filled her mouth. She hadn't drunk vodka for years. Jules didn't like it. She'd said it reminded her of alcoholics and teenagers and insisted gin was a much more suitable drink. Not that she really liked Cally drinking. For Jules, her body was her temple, and she didn't put anything in it her dietitian hadn't written on her plan. Early on in their relationship, she'd paid for Cally to have a consultation with the same dietician, who scribbled down a soul-destroying list of acceptable foods that mostly consisted of green vegetables and boiled chicken. Cally should have known then the relationship was doomed.

It wasn't like Cally was a big foodie, but she enjoyed potatoes and bread and cheese and cake. And the occasional vodka.

Cally realised the butcher had been speaking for a while now and she hadn't heard a word he'd said. Luckily he didn't seem to notice. Cally nodded with what she thought was an approximation of polite interest. She probably would want him to supply food to the glamping site if he came in at the right price, but tonight she decided she was going to try to just have a nice time and make a good impression. Behind her, she heard the whine of feedback as someone plugged in a guitar. She turned to see the band setting up on the tiny stage at the far end of the pub.

From her left, someone grabbed her arm. "Oh, for Christ's sake, Colin, leave the poor woman alone. You're boring the arse off her."

Cally looked at the woman who grabbed her arm. The butcher—Colin—looked sheepish. "Just talking a bit of business, Sian."

"Well, she looks ready to top herself, so give it a rest." The woman looked at Cally. Cally recognised her as the woman from the meeting who'd spent the whole thing staring at her. A wave of uneasiness washed over her before it was completely obliterated when the woman gave her a big grin and said, "I'm Sian, and I own the bakery. I thought you were brilliant today, and we're all excited about your new place. I'll be bending your ear soon about business, but tonight we've got the Great Danes doing their horrendous covers on the stage, and I want to dance."

Cally didn't know what to say back to this tiny ball of energy. Sian was about four feet eleven and could probably fit into kids' clothes, but she was surprisingly strong when she clamped down on Cally's arm and dragged her over to the dance floor. Cally allowed herself to be pulled along and even to enjoy herself a little. The Great Danes had struck up a catchy old pop song you couldn't help at least tap your foot to. Before Jules, Cally had liked to dance. She hoped she still remembered how.

Sian elbowed a few people out of the way and made some room for them in the middle of the dance floor. No one seemed to mind, and most smiled at her. She leaned close to Cally to be heard over the music. "I've decided we're going to be friends. You were just so awesome today. Hopefully you're okay with that."

Cally laughed. She hadn't had a friend in so long. She nodded. "Okay."

"Good. Otherwise I guess I'd just be a stalker," Sian said and moved away again.

The next song started without a pause, and Cally let herself go. She let herself consider that maybe she could have a good life here. It wouldn't be anything fancy or exciting, but it would be hers. If she was lucky, maybe she'd make a few friends, enjoy her work, and be content, at peace. It wouldn't be the life she had before, and Cally was relieved at that. That life had been miserable and lonely and full of anxiety and fear. Maybe Halesbrook could be a place she could be happy.

Obviously, that idiot Laurie was a bit of a fly in the ointment, but Cally could deal with her. Besides, she wasn't here tonight. After everything she'd said earlier, she hadn't bothered to turn up. Probably had a better offer. She didn't strike Cally as the most reliable—after all, she'd made a big deal about speaking at the meeting and then hadn't. Cally tried not to dwell on the fact she had scanned the room a couple of times to see if Laurie was in the pub. And she *really* didn't want to think about why that made her feel a little disappointment.

Before she could think any more about it, Sian leaned towards her, fanned her face, and mimed getting a drink. Cally thought that was a great idea.

The bar was crowded, but Sian muscled a few people out the way. They seemed to take it well. Sian shouted to be heard over the noise. "Gin?"

Cally shook her head. "No. Vodka, please."

Sian nodded her approval and turned away to order. As she did, Cally felt someone push into her back from behind. The smell of alcohol was like a cloud around her head as she felt them lean into her ear. "I know who you are."

Cally turned into the stench and the woman who stood right behind her. "What did you say?"

The woman swayed and poked Cally in her chest. "I *know* who you are."

"Good for you," Cally said and turned away again.

The woman pushed into Cally again and put a hand on her shoulder to try to turn her around. That pissed Cally off. She swung back around so quickly the woman nearly fell backwards. "What?" Cally asked.

"You killed that poor woman with your lies. You're evil," the woman slurred and swayed again.

Cally couldn't breathe. She wanted to tell this drunk woman to fuck off, to say she didn't know what she was talking about. But she couldn't get air into her lungs, let alone speak. Cally had to get out of there.

She pushed past the people around the bar, not caring how rude she looked. She shoved her way to the door and almost fell out the doors. Outside, Cally bent over at the waist and dragged air into her lungs. She wobbled on her legs, and the world went hazy for a moment.

She gritted her teeth and told herself not to faint, not to embarrass herself like that. When she could breathe again, Cally walked a little ways down the road and crouched in a doorway.

She heard the low buzz from the pub become a roar for a second as the door opened and closed again. Cally gritted her teeth and prayed it wasn't the drunk woman coming out for round two.

"Cally?" It was Sian. She didn't know whether to be relieved or not. "Cally?"

"Over here," Cally called from the doorway.

The click clack of heels and Sian was standing in front of her. "You all right?"

Cally nodded. "Yes, fine. Just needed some air."

Sian nodded and crouched down. "Someone said Lara Michaels was talking to you."

"I don't know who that is," Cally said, which was the truth, but she guessed the drunk woman was Lara Michaels.

"She's a dick," Sian said simply, and Cally couldn't help but laugh. "She *is.* Someone said she accosted you while we were getting drinks."

"We were a bit of a spectacle, then?" Cally asked with dread. That was the last thing she wanted. Damn that stupid drunk woman for bringing attention to her.

"Not at all," Sian said and rubbed Cally's arm. "Look, most people know who you are."

Cally closed her eyes. She opened them again when Sian squeezed her arm. "Cally—Cally, look at me."

Cally did.

"Just because it's known doesn't mean anyone cares. I only came here recently myself. But people are nice. If you give them a chance, they'll give you one. And trust me, no one cares what Lara Michaels thinks. She'll probably be kicked out in the next half an hour anyway."

"I think I'm going to go home," Cally said.

"Why?"

"You know why."

Sian shook her head angrily. "Don't let her chase you off. Don't let her give anyone a reason to think you're ashamed."

Cally sighed. She was so tired of this. "Sian, I don't care what people think."

Sian nodded. "Then come back inside. If you don't care, prove it."

"What's the point?"

"This is a small town. If you really want to make your business a success, you need to be friendly with people," Sian said in an almost exact copy of what Laurie told her earlier. "People will talk because that's what they do. You need to front it. And if you let someone like Lara Michaels chase you off, you won't last five minutes."

Cally knew Sian had a point. Who was this Lara Michaels to Cally anyway? She didn't know her, and it didn't sound like she was massively respected anyway. "You're sure she'll be kicked out in the next half hour?" Cally asked.

Sian grinned and crossed her heart. "Swear it. It's the same every weekend."

Cally made herself smile even though she still felt a bit sick.

"I'll be your bodyguard. I won't let her near you," Sian said.

"I thought you said she'll be kicked out soon."

"She will. But I mean until then. I'll watch you like a hawk," Sian said.

"Fine." Cally let Sian pull her up. She really was strong. "But if she's not out in half an hour—"

"We'll go to yours and get smashed," Sian said and Cally laughed.

They went back inside, and true to Sian's word, Lara Michaels was kicked out within ten minutes for falling on a table and knocking over a load of drinks.

Chapter Eight

Sian giggled and Cally snorted when she dropped her car keys in the gutter for the third time.

"I'll get them," Sian said and staggered into a kind of crouch by the kerb.

Cally snorted again and dropped ungracefully to her knees beside her. "No, you're too drunk. *I'll* get them. Move over." Cally bumped Sian's shoulder, and they both fell sideways laughing.

"We are *so* drunk," Sian said.

"*So* drunk," Cally said. "I'll get us an Uber."

Sian burst out laughing. "Are you mad? There's no Ubers out here."

"How are we even going to get home? Are there cabs?"

"Not really. I didn't really think about getting home. Whoops," Sian said and laughed. "Oh shit. I'll have to call Nick."

Cally tried to remember who Nick was and came up short. "Nick. Okay, call Nick," she said. "Got them." Cally snagged her keys, which were slippery as fuck and kept moving about in the gutter. She used the car for support and managed to stand up. "Bingo," she said as she finally managed to press the lock release on her car keys. She'd left her house keys in the car—old habit—so she wouldn't lose them. Not the best idea when she was so drunk.

"Hope you two aren't driving." Laurie.

"Hey, Laurie," Sian said and stumbled over to her. Laurie barely caught her before she toppled over.

"Hi, Sian. Cally."

"Laurie," Cally said, trying to sound sober but knowing she was failing miserably.

"We're drunk, Laurie," Sian said and giggled.

"I can see that, Sian," Laurie replied.

"Can you give us a lift to Cally's house? We're having a sleepover."

Laurie raised an eyebrow and looked at Cally. "You move fast."

Cally rolled her eyes. Even drunk as she was, she still found Laurie irritating. "I need to get my keys out of my car." Cally ignored Laurie's childish comment. "I had no intention of driving."

"Relax, I was only kidding. I'll take you home. Want me to get your keys out of your car? Probably not a good idea for you to do it."

Cally nodded. Getting into her car this drunk even though she would never have driven drunk wouldn't be a good look if the police or anyone else happened along. She handed Laurie the keys. "Thanks. They're in the glove compartment."

"No problem. My truck's unlocked—you can go and get in. Unless you need help?" Laurie's smirk was back.

"We're fine," Cally said.

"No, Cally, we aren't," Sian said. "We're really, *really* drunk."

It was bad enough they had to rely on Laurie for a lift home. Cally was not going to be led to her truck like some…some *drunk*.

"Come on, Sian." Cally linked arms with Sian, feeling a little more sober. They made their way slowly to Laurie's truck.

"Hey, Cally. Where did you say your keys were again?" Laurie called.

"In the glove compartment," Cally called back.

"I checked there."

Cally huffed. "Well you didn't check properly, then. I always leave them there," she said loudly. Great. Now anyone listening knew where she kept her keys. She supposed she was still pretty drunk.

Laurie came over. "I promise they aren't there. Did you maybe take them into the pub with you by accident?"

"No."

"Well, then you've lost them," Laurie said.

Cally pushed past her and walked—kind of staggered a bit like people who are pretending to be sober do—and looked in the glove compartment. Fuck. Laurie was right. They weren't there.

"Maybe you did take them into the pub and they fell out of your bag," Laurie said.

"Or maybe someone stole my car key out of my bag and got them out of my car," Cally said and immediately realised how stupid that sounded.

"You have your car key," Laurie said.

"Maybe they put it back." Cally couldn't stop herself.

"Well, either way, you have no keys. How are you going to get in?" Laurie asked.

Cally didn't know. Her head was starting to hurt, which was just great. Early onset hangover.

"Look, I'll drive you back, and we can see if there's an open window or something," Laurie said.

"There isn't. I always lock up," Cally replied.

"Well, let's just see," Laurie said. "If you can't get in, I can drive you out to Sian's. Or you can stay at mine."

"What are you even doing out so late?" Cally asked. "You didn't go to the pub."

"I couldn't sleep, so I went for a drive," Laurie said and walked Cally back to her truck. "Lucky for you."

Was it, though? Cally wondered.

Chapter Nine

Sian had fallen asleep in the back of Laurie's truck, and Cally's headache was building fast. She thought she might be sick and prayed Laurie would be gone before that happened. Surely she deserved to keep some modicum of her dignity.

"Right," Laurie said. "I'll check the windows to see if you left any open or unlocked on the ground floor. They're sash, so it happens more than you think."

"I didn't leave a window open. I'm very careful about security," Cally said. Laurie looked at her but didn't say anything. She didn't need to—Cally knew what she was thinking. Careful about security and yet here they were at one in the morning trying to break into Cally's house because she lost her keys.

Cally followed Laurie out of the truck. "You should stay in there where it's warm. I won't be long."

Cally shook her head. "It's my house, so I'll help."

Laurie rolled her eyes. "Fine but be careful—it's muddy."

"I *know* it's muddy, I *live* here. *You* be careful," Cally said and cringed at how childish she sounded. Fuck it. Laurie was an annoying know-it-all, and Cally didn't even like her.

For the second time in as many days, Cally wished she had a decent outside light.

"You should think about some security lights," Laurie said, switching on a torch that appeared from nowhere. "It gets dark out in the country. And very spooky at night." She held the torch under her chin and made a stupid face. Cally laughed before she could stop herself.

They squelched up to the front of the house. "Hang on a minute," Laurie said and shone the torch at the door.

Cally's heart sank immediately. Well, at least she'd found her keys. They were in the door. And the door was wide open.

Laurie turned to her, and Cally expected a smart remark and that infuriating smirk. She was surprised when she got neither. Laurie looked worried. "Did you leave it like this?"

Cally's throat was dry and her face was hot. She felt sick and didn't know if it was the alcohol or the embarrassment over what she'd done. "I don't think so." Her voice sounded weak and unsure and she hated it. She took a deep breath. "I don't think I would have done that."

"But you aren't sure?" Laurie asked.

"No," admitted Cally. "I'm not sure." She'd had a lot on her mind lately. Only this morning she'd forgotten to lock the front door. But she'd *realised* it as soon as she'd driven away. "I'm pretty sure I didn't—wouldn't—leave the keys in it like that."

Laurie nodded. "But you could have?"

"I already said that, didn't I?" Cally snapped. "Sorry. I know you're trying to help. It's just…"

"Yeah, I know," Laurie said. "We should probably have a look around and make sure you haven't been robbed. I mean, it's unlikely, but you never know."

By now, apart from her banging headache and roiling stomach, Cally was stone cold sober. The air helped. It was damp and fresh and smelled of the earth. It helped to breathe it in and settled her stomach.

"Let's go, then," Cally said and stepped up to the front door.

"Hang on. Look, don't get annoyed again, but you're pretty drunk. Maybe I should go on my own," Laurie said.

"Thanks for your concern, but I'm fine and I'm coming," Cally said.

Laurie sighed and moved up behind Cally. She shone the torch into the hall. Fine so far. The rug and the hall table were undisturbed. Cally half expected big muddy footprints.

"Christ, it's cold in here," Laurie said.

"The front door's been open all night," Cally said. She turned on her phone torch and shone it at the thermostat. Back down to ten again. What the fuck?

"You okay?" Laurie asked.

"Yes. It's just…the thermostat. I never have it down that low," Cally said. "It did the same yesterday."

"Might be a fault. Come on, let's go inside," Laurie said and brushed past Cally to go in first. She reached out and flicked the light switch. Nothing.

That was not good. Cally was the first to admit her electrics were shit, but they'd never not worked. Fear settled somewhere in the middle of her chest. Something about this was all wrong. She wondered if Laurie felt it too. All the same, this was *her* place and she wouldn't be frightened away.

"It's my house—I should go first," Cally said.

"Really? Why do you have to argue with me about everything?" Laurie asked.

"Because you're bloody bossy," Cally said and pushed past Laurie. She held her phone out in front of her. It didn't give as good a light as Laurie's torch, but it would do.

Cally walked down the hall towards the kitchen. As they got close, they heard a noise coming from the other side of the door. Cally took a step back, afraid. What the hell was that?

"Can you hear that?" she whispered.

"Yeah," Laurie whispered back. "What is it?"

Cally didn't know. Something crashed to the floor on the other side of the door and made them both jump. Laurie dropped her torch and it skittered away.

"Shit," Laurie said. "We should go back outside and call the police."

"No," Cally said. "It's my house." Before she could change her mind, she pushed open the door. Another crash, and then something came at her, fast. Cally screamed.

Chapter Ten

Cally jumped back, stumbled, and fell into Laurie. They both went down onto the hall floor. The thing that had jumped at her ran past, and Cally felt it brush her arm.

"What the fuck was that?" Cally pushed the words out on a breath. Her chest was tight. Was this what it felt like to have a heart attack? Behind her, underneath her, Laurie started to laugh.

"Oh my God, oh my God, I think I shit my pants," Laurie wheezed.

"Why are you *laughing*?" Cally hissed.

"It was a dog. A fucking dog. Oh my God, I thought we were dead," Laurie said.

"A dog?"

"A dog. Just a dog." Laurie helped Cally to her feet. "Christ, that really had me going." Laurie went back down the hall and picked up her torch. She aimed it at the kitchen doorway. "See? It must have knocked some stuff over, looking for food. Probably the stray a few people have mentioned seeing."

Cally took a deep breath. Just a dog. It must have wandered in because the front door was wide open all evening. If someone had once owned it, maybe it had a memory of houses being safe, warm places with food. Poor bloody thing.

"Where's your fuse box?" Laurie asked. "Please don't say the basement."

Cally laughed. "No, it's here in the hall. In that cupboard." She pointed to a door under the stairs.

Laurie opened it and fiddled around with something, Cally had no idea what. Suddenly, the hall light came on.

"Blew a fuse," Laurie said. "Not uncommon in an old house. Plus your electrics look like antiques."

Cally couldn't argue. But still, it all seemed like such a coincidence. Leaving the keys in the door, fuses blowing, and the thermostat…

"We should have a quick look around anyway. Make sure there isn't another Mr. Dog rooting around in your underwear drawer upstairs," Laurie said.

They checked the living room, the bathroom, bedrooms, and even the loft. Everything was undisturbed and just as she'd left it earlier. Cally guessed she couldn't really deny that she'd left the key in the front door. She felt foolish. Laurie must think she was a right idiot.

Not that she cared what Laurie thought.

They finished up back in the hall downstairs. "I guess I'd better get Sleeping Drunky out of the car and leave you in peace, then," Laurie said.

Cally nodded. "Thanks for tonight. I promise, I'm not as ditzy as I must seem."

Laurie smiled. "I didn't think you were. No one who can give a presentation like you did earlier could be ditzy. Leaving keys in the door"—Laurie shrugged—"happens to the best of us."

Cally smiled. So Laurie could be nice. Who knew? "Thanks."

"Welcome. Want to help me get Cindersozzled out of the truck?" Laurie asked.

"Stop calling her names." Cally laughed. "I'll help, though. It's the least I can do."

"Sian's a good egg. And she does a mean cheese twist. But she can't handle her booze. I've lost count of the number of times I've poured her into the back of my truck and driven her home."

"You know her well, then?" Cally asked and was surprised by the tiny pang of jealousy.

"Not really well. She only came here shortly before you. Made quite an impression, though. And she's lovely, so I don't mind being her taxi from time to time."

She and Laurie walked back outside. Somewhere in the distance an owl hooted.

"Cold," Cally said and crossed her arms around her middle. "Let's do this quickly—it's freezing."

Now that all the excitement was over, Cally's headache was really starting to kick in, and she was dreading the hangover tomorrow—well, today, actually. It was already close to two in the morning.

"No worries," said Laurie. "I wouldn't mind getting to my bed either. I've got—Hey, what's going on?"

At first, Cally didn't know what Laurie was talking about. It was so dark, and they were relying on Laurie's torch again. She followed the beam of light as Laurie shone it over the ground. Then she saw it. Laurie's two front tyres were flat—completely flat, and one was torn open.

"Shit," Laurie said and quickly walked around the truck. "What the *fuck*? At least the back two are okay."

Cally approached the truck. There was a strange light and airy feeling in her middle, like her stomach had vacated. She guessed it had. It was sitting somewhere around her throat. "Jesus, Laurie," she whispered.

"What shit luck that is. I didn't even notice when we were coming up. I have one spare but not two."

Sian. Cally hoped she was all right. She had to check.

Cally's stomach dropped hard back into her middle, and she opened the door on her side.

Sian was lying in the back seat with her coat over her, snoring softly. Cally breathed deeply. Okay, at least she was all right. For a second there, Cally had visions of Sian…well, it didn't matter.

Laurie opened the truck door on her side and looked at Cally through the truck. "We should get her inside. We should all get inside—it's bloody freezing. You mind if I call the breakdown people from yours?"

Cally nodded. "Sure." Laurie didn't seem too bothered. A bit annoyed maybe, but not scared. Not like Cally was scared. It was happening again.

Chapter Eleven

With Sian safely asleep on the sofa in the living room, Cally wondered how much to tell Laurie. After all, she barely knew her, and she'd hoped this thing wouldn't follow her all the way to Halesbrook. She'd been so careful. But how much to say?

"I'll pay for your tyres," Cally said as they sat at her kitchen table.

Laurie looked at Cally over the hot mug of tea. "Why would you do that?"

"Well, because it happened on my property."

"So? I probably drove over something on the way up here. Your drive is a disaster zone. I did feel something bump under the wheels on the way up. Must have been that," Laurie said.

"That's what I mean. You wouldn't have been driving up here if we weren't so drunk. Please, let me pay. I feel bad," Cally said.

As soon as they put Sian on the sofa, Cally went straight back into the hall and locked the front door. She'd quickly glanced outside before closing the door but it was pointless. Way too dark to see anything—anyone. She shivered.

"Look, I appreciate it, but it's fine. Honestly. It's happened before. I drive that truck all over the forest. Sometimes my tyres puncture."

Cally nodded. She wasn't going to argue further, wasn't going to draw attention to herself. Besides, maybe Laurie was right and she had driven over something. After Jules died, and all that other stuff happened, Cally got used to living in a constant state of anxiety. Maybe this was exactly what Laurie seemed to think it was.

Cally felt herself relax a little. Nothing had happened since she moved here, and people got flat tyres all the time. Besides, how likely was it someone was lurking around out here, waiting for them?

She was tired, and her hangover had kicked in, and she wasn't thinking straight. Why drag up the past with Laurie now? What was the point?

"Cally? Earth to Cally? You okay?" Laurie asked.

"Sorry, yes—yes, I'm fine. Hangover has gone to work, that's all," Cally said.

"Why don't you go to bed? I can pull the door shut behind me when the recovery bloke turns up," Laurie said and stood. She gathered the mugs off the table and took them to the sink.

"No, I can't do that," Cally said and stood up. "Here, let me take those. They can go in the dishwasher."

Laurie handed Cally the mugs and leaned back against the kitchen counter. "Are you sure you're okay?"

Cally busied herself with moving stuff around in the dishwasher so she wouldn't have to look at Laurie, wouldn't give anything away. "I'm sure. Just tired and drunk. It's been a really long day."

"Yeah. Lots going on for you. Look, go to bed, honestly. I promise not to steal anything," Laurie said, and Cally laughed.

Cally turned as Laurie put her hand on her shoulder. "I trust you," Cally said, then realised that was a lie. She hadn't trusted anyone for a long time.

"No, you don't, but that's okay. You don't really know me yet," Laurie said and took her hand away.

"Yet?" Cally asked.

Laurie nodded. "We're going to be good friends, you and I."

"Are we now? You're the second person who's said that tonight."

"That's because we're a very friendly village."

Cally grinned and felt the lingering fear from earlier leave her. "We don't even like each other."

"Don't we? I'm wounded. You don't like me?" Laurie said.

"No, not a bit. You were so annoying earlier," Cally said.

"That's rude. I think I *will* let you pay for my tyres," Laurie said.

"No, I've decided to call it even. I saved your life, remember?" Cally said.

"My life is worth two tyres to you?"

"At a push," Cally said and grinned. She noticed now they were standing close, really close. Laurie must have noticed too because she took a step back and cleared her throat.

"Well…" Laurie said.

Cally heard the sound of an engine outside. "Looks like your breakdown assistance is here."

Laurie nodded. "It does. Unless you're expecting another new friend."

Cally shook her head. "No."

"Okay, well, I'll let you get to bed, then."

Cally nodded. "I'll walk you out."

Cally followed Laurie to the front door and almost bumped into her when she pulled up short.

"You locked us in?" Laurie turned to Cally, looking puzzled.

Cally walked around her and twisted the deadbolt back. "Old habits." She said it brightly, trying to sound like before when they'd been messing about in the kitchen. It sounded hollow to her own ears, though. "I'm from London." As if that explained it, which she guessed it did to a certain extent.

"London. Yeah, I think I heard that," Laurie said. "Well, I guess I'll come back later and take you to collect your car."

"Oh." Cally hadn't even thought about how she'd get her car. She wasn't used to there being no taxis. "You don't have to. Sian mentioned a boyfriend or husband or whatever, before. Nick? He might be able to drop me."

Laurie turned in the doorway and that smirk was back. "Ah yes, the elusive Nick. Okay, well, if you change your mind, let me know."

"How will I let you know?" Cally asked, letting the Nick thing go. There was obviously something there, but she was too tired to get into it.

"Give me your phone," Laurie said.

"No. I'm not giving you my phone," Cally said.

Laurie rolled her eyes. "To write my number in."

"Oh. Oh yes, of course." Cally unlocked her phone and sheepishly held it out. "Sorry."

Laurie quickly put her number in, turned, and was gone. Cally locked up and looked around her hall. It was the same as always.

Nothing moved or gone. She'd do a proper look in the morning, but for now, she needed to sleep. She checked the thermostat and was relieved it hadn't gone back down. She'd need to get that sorted.

She turned off the lights downstairs, did a quick check on Sian, who was still out for the count on her sofa, and went to bed.

Chapter Twelve

Eighteen months ago

"Give me your phone, Cally. I'm not going to ask again."

Cally held it out, and Jules snatched it away.

"PIN." It wasn't a question. "I know you changed it. What's the fucking PIN?"

Cally told Jules and then braced herself. Not because there was anything on there she was ashamed of—she wasn't that stupid. But Jules would find *something*. Cally knew she would. She already knew Jules had a tracker on her phone. Knew where Cally was every minute of every bloody day. Jules controlled the bank accounts and could see every transaction Cally made. Even so, even with all that, she got it in her head from time to time that Cally was up to something. That was how she put it. *I know you're up to something—let me see your phone.*

At first, in the early days, Cally had believed Jules when she told Cally her last girlfriend had cheated, and now she had trust issues. In the early days, Cally couldn't *wait* to let Jules look through her phone, to reassure her, to show Jules that she was different. That she was loyal.

Now it was just another lock on her prison door. A constant reminder that she wasn't free to look at what she wanted, even in her internet searches. Jules would go through them with a fine-tooth comb. They were usually the source of their disagreements. Before, it had been Cally's friends, but they were all gone. The ones Jules hadn't seen off had drifted away of their own accord. Cally didn't blame them. You couldn't be friends with someone you never saw, someone who cancelled plans last minute or always, *always* brought her girlfriend along.

And Jules would not make it fun. She'd sit there stony-faced and rude. They'd leave early. What was the point?

And now Cally sat on their super-king-sized bed and waited.

"Who's Pete? Why are you asking him to come over?" Jules glanced up from Cally's phone. "Well?"

Cally searched her memory. Who the fuck was Pete? "I don't—oh, hang on. The plumber. Last week when the washing machine packed up." Cally felt the relief wash over her. It was like she was on a game show. *For two thousand pounds, who's Pete?*

Jules had been here. She'd met him. Thank God.

Jules grunted. "He overcharged us."

He hadn't. He'd been fair and fixed the washing machine. Jules had stood over him, watching, the whole time. It was embarrassing.

"You know I don't like doing this, Cally. You know I don't," Jules said.

She did. She did like doing it. Except *like* wasn't the right word. Cally didn't know what it was. She couldn't understand any of it. When she tried to think about it, about how she'd ended up here, it made her head hurt, made her want to lie down and sleep. How had she gotten herself in such a mess?

"I knew it." Jules looked triumphant. Cally's heart sank. "Why the fuck are you speaking to Caitlyn?"

Cally knew by now that trying to explain was pointless. It didn't matter. Jules wanted to find something, and she did. Cally braced herself. She knew what was coming next, and she asked herself again, why? How did she get here?

And then it began.

Chapter Thirteen

Now

Cally managed four hours' sleep. When she woke up, her mouth felt like a litter tray—not that she'd ever had a cat, or tasted a litter tray. She reached for her phone and saw two texts, the most she'd had at one time since Jules used to bombard her back in the bad old days. She'd check them once she'd showered and dressed.

Cally forced herself up and out of bed. Her head thudded and her stomach sloshed. She waited for a moment—then, when she was sure she wouldn't throw up, she went into the bathroom.

She turned the shower on hot, as hot as it would go, and brushed her teeth as the steam quickly fogged the mirror. She wasn't sure if Sian was still there or not. She hadn't heard her moving around downstairs but guessed she could still be asleep on the sofa.

Cally stepped under the spray and sighed as the hot water soaked her. That was one thing about this house, it might be falling down around her ears but the water pressure was amazing.

Showered and dressed and with her mouth tasting less terrible, Cally went downstairs. She poked her head around the living room door. No Sian. She wasn't in the kitchen either. "Damn," Cally muttered under her breath. She was hoping for a lift back into the village to pick up her car.

Cally checked her phone and saw the first message was from Sian. It thanked her for sorting her out the night before and said Nick had come early to pick her up. Sian also said she'd asked Laurie to come and get Cally. Great. Why had Sian done that when Cally could just have easily walked? It would have taken about an hour, but maybe the exercise would do her good.

Cally checked the other message. Laurie. She said to message when she was ready for a lift. Cally started to type that she wouldn't need a lift, then changed her mind. She really wasn't feeling good. The phone buzzed in her hand. Another message. Cally read it and laughed out loud. It was Laurie telling her not to even think about walking because she'd most likely end up getting squashed by a tractor.

Cally sighed and told Laurie she was ready whenever Laurie was free. The phone buzzed again almost instantly. Laurie would be over in an hour.

Cally went into the kitchen and put the kettle on. Last night Laurie told her they were going to be friends. Cally wasn't sure how she felt about that. In the space of a day, Cally went from hating her guts to getting texts off her. It was all moving so fast. She supposed it wouldn't hurt to be friendly, and so far Laurie hadn't given the impression she was after anything more. Cally guessed time would tell. She *hoped* Laurie wasn't after anything more because Cally had sworn off women after Jules. Relationships, she decided, weren't for her. Not if there was the possibility of ending up the same way.

Logically, Cally knew Jules wasn't the norm, but she'd started off charming and sweet and given no clue as to the monster lurking beneath. Not that Cally thought Laurie was necessarily the same—even early on Jules had a forceful personality. But Cally didn't trust herself. Besides, Laurie had offered friendship, nothing more. Cally decided to take her at her word and see how it went.

True to her word, Laurie arrived at Cally's house an hour later. "How did you sleep?" Laurie asked.

"Got four hours," Cally said.

Laurie winced. "Ouch. You must be knackered."

Cally nodded. "I don't feel great. Thanks for coming to get me."

"No bother. Sian texted me."

"Yes, she left before I got up. I feel bad. I didn't offer her tea or anything," Cally said.

"Oh, I wouldn't worry about it. She probably went home to sleep it off some more."

"Probably a good idea. I don't think my sofa's so comfortable," Cally said. "Looks like you got your tyres sorted."

"I did. They were able to repair one of them."

"Are you sure I can't pay for them?" Cally asked.

Laurie shook her head. "No, put it towards getting your drive tarmacked."

Cally laughed. "That is pretty much last on my list."

"Yeah, you've got all those cabins to build, I guess," Laurie said quietly.

"Why are you so against it?" Cally asked, trying to remember Laurie was doing her a favour here and not get defensive.

"I said already. I don't think it'll be good for the forest. All the extra rubbish and traffic," Laurie said.

"Right, but what do you think will happen to the forest if there's no tourists to come and see it?" Cally asked.

"What do you mean?"

"Well, I imagine you make most of your money from parking and memberships and the cafes."

"Yeah."

"So if there's no tourists, then who's spending their money in your precious forest?" Cally asked.

Laurie laughed. "My precious forest? Look, I take your point, but there's plenty of hotels and B-and-Bs around. They'll still come. They just don't need to stay *in* the forest. We're considering taking it to a judicial review, by the way. To get the approval reversed."

Cally felt like the air had gone out of her. She felt betrayed, which was stupid because Laurie didn't owe her anything, but even so… "Stop the truck, please," Cally said as calmly as she could.

"What?" Laurie glanced over at her.

"I said, stop the truck."

"Why? It's still another half-hour walk," Laurie said.

"I don't care. Please stop the truck."

Laurie indicated and pulled over to the side of the road. "Look, Cally, this isn't personal."

Cally laughed hard and sharp. "It feels very personal. I'm supposed to sign contracts in a few days. I can't if you try to get the planning repealed, can I?"

"It's not personal. We'd do the same whoever it was. I'd like to think we can still be friends," Laurie said.

Cally opened the truck door and got out. Before she slammed it shut, she leaned back inside. "My first impression of you was right. You are arrogant and conceited. Not personal? *All* my life savings are in Five Oaks. *All* of it. So you saying it's not personal doesn't really help me. You've decided you don't want more tourists because of your forest, and fuck everyone else, all the local businesses that'll die, not to mention my place."

Laurie reached out to touch Cally's hand, which rested on the passenger seat, and Cally snatched it away. "Don't."

"Cally, I'm sorry. I mean, you already have cabins and pitches up there. Can't they be enough? Do you need to make the place even bigger? Surely what you've got will make a good little business."

"A *good little business*? Oh, fuck off, you patronising twat." Cally slammed the truck door and stepped back. Furious, she walked away without looking back. How bloody dare she. *Good little business*? How arrogant and condescending. She worked in a forest, for fuck's sake. What did she know about business?

Cally heard the sound of Laurie's truck get quieter as it drove away. She tried to remember which side of the road you were supposed to walk on when there were no pavements.

Just then, the heavens opened, rain poured down heavy and hard, and Cally was soaked almost instantly. Her headache was back. She blamed Laurie for all of it. Rainwater quickly began to collect in puddles along the verge, and Cally's feet were soon as soaked as the rest of her. Great. Perfect.

The forest loomed over Cally on each side of the road, thick with fir and oak and beech and chestnut. The first time Cally came up here, she was blown away. Twenty-seven thousand acres big, someone told her. She ran its paths and trails most days and was starting to learn her small section of it and fall in love with it even more each time. Today, though, it was an ominous thing, and she wasn't sure why—she guessed the rain and the fight with Laurie—but today, instead of making her feel free, the sight of it closing in on her from either side made Cally feel claustrophobic.

It pushed in at her from each side, and it was impossible to see between the trees. The gaps there were dark and unwelcoming. From her left, Cally caught a flash of orange. She stopped and squinted into the forest. There was nothing there.

She picked up her pace again and carried on walking. The sky had gone dark, and Cally guessed it was going to be a miserable sort of day.

There it was again, that flash of orange. Cally stopped and called out.

"Hello?" Silence. "Is anyone there?"

She waited a moment. No one appeared. Cally felt a coldness that had nothing to do with the weather settle inside her. Maybe she was being paranoid, but it felt like someone was following her. Suddenly, she realised how vulnerable she was out here on a country road. No cars had been past at all, and all around her were twenty-seven thousand acres of forest and not a soul in sight.

Cally walked on. She focused on picking up her pace and getting into the village as quickly as possible.

Cally estimated she probably had another twenty minutes of walking. She kept her head turned slightly to the side, so she could see if the orange thing made another appearance.

Cally tried to think of what it could be if it wasn't a person and came up empty. There was no animal in nature—certainly not in the UK—that was bright orange. But then, if someone *was* following her, why would they wear such a bright colour to do it?

Because they wanted her to know.

Cally felt her stomach tighten. She thought back to the letters she was still receiving. Nasty, poisonous letters. She'd spent a fortune on private investigations to try to figure out who was sending them but had no joy. They'd been coming since Jules died. They knew things about her. Then there were the other things that happened before she left London for good.

Since the move, she now only got the letters through redirected post. That was a relief because it meant whoever was sending them didn't know her well enough to have her new address. Even so, that didn't mean they hadn't found out. Were they now waiting for her in the forest? Following her and waiting for an opportunity?

She told herself to stop being ridiculous. She'd started getting the letters nine months ago. The person sending them knew where she lived. Even if they had decided one day to do something to her, why would they follow her all the way up here and wait in a forest for her to walk past? She was alone all the time. They were still sending the letters to her old address. *This*, Cally decided, was nothing to do with *that*. *This* might not even be anything. Just paranoid old Cally again.

There it was again, that flash of orange. This time Cally stopped and turn to face where it had been. "I know you're there. Why don't you come out, you fucking weirdo," she shouted. Her voice was strong, and that pleased her. It reverberated into the forest. "Come on. Instead of following me, you coward."

Someone stepped out of the forest. The orange she'd seen was their jacket with the hood pulled down over their head so Cally couldn't see their face. Her heart beat fast, and she tried to keep the panic from overwhelming her.

The figure just stood there, facing Cally. She didn't know what to do. "What do you want?" she called out and heard the change in her voice and hated the fear she heard there.

"Who are you?"

The figure was about twenty feet away and stared at her. She took two steps back, getting ready to run.

The figure in the orange jacket took two steps towards her.

Cally turned and ran.

Chapter Fourteen

Nine months ago

Jules had been standing out there for fifteen minutes at least. At first Cally thought she was going to knock on the door and waited inside with dread. But she'd been out there, just standing on the pavement, over the road and didn't look like she had any plans to come over.

Since Cally left Jules, strange things had been happening. Calls in the middle of the night with no one on the other end. Nasty messages on social media from made-up accounts. Childish, petty things. Cally ignored them all. She didn't report it because she hoped Jules would stop once she realised Cally wasn't coming back to her.

At first, Jules had tried charm. She'd promised to change. Promised Cally the house in the countryside she'd always wanted. New car, new wardrobe, holidays, anything and everything, until she'd finally begged. Got down on her knees and actually begged Cally, who'd been horrified. Cally still said no, and then Jules changed. Jules became… scary. Cally thought maybe it had something to do with the begging, that maybe Jules couldn't cope with the idea she'd got on her knees and Cally still said no. The balance of power had shifted, and Jules couldn't deal with it.

Anyway, whatever it was, Jules was now standing opposite Cally's house and Cally wasn't totally sure what to do about it. It wasn't like Jules was trying to hide it. She was just standing there, looking at Cally's house in that ridiculous orange jacket.

Cally had an idea that maybe she should call the police—but what would she say? *My ex is standing outside my house doing nothing*?

Of course, she knew it was weird and she had a suspicion that with the calls and the messages and now the standing outside her house, it would probably be called harassment, but Cally couldn't quite make herself report Jules. She thought a therapist would be able to tell her what that was all about, but Cally hadn't been to one. Something about feeling embarrassed and—laughably—like she was betraying Jules.

Her biggest fear, though, in the dead of night when she couldn't get back to sleep, was that if she told anyone, *really* told the whole story about life with Jules, she'd be told she'd deserved everything. That it was her fault. That she really had driven Jules to behave the way she did, just like Jules always told her.

In the morning, Cally knew that was nonsense, that she hadn't deserved any of it, that Jules was probably either quite unwell or quite fucking evil. But there was a little voice in Cally's head that stopped her telling, and at night, that little voice got loud.

Cally sighed. What the bloody hell was she going to do? She couldn't just leave Jules standing out there. What if she never left? What if she was still there tonight when Cally went to bed. She shivered. *That* didn't bear thinking about.

Cally sneaked another look out the window, fully expecting Jules to still be there. She was gone. Cally looked up and down the road. No sign of her.

Downstairs, she thought she heard the sound of the back door open. It had a squeaky hinge she hadn't gotten around to oiling. Cally stepped away from the window. She thought about pushing the sofa in front of the door, but the floors were wood and the sofa wasn't that heavy. She didn't think it would hold off whoever—*Jules*—for long.

Could she make it out the front door? No. The kitchen was only a couple of metres from the locked front door. She'd never make it, let alone unlock the door in time.

Could she go out the window? They were sash, and she could climb through. Cally pinched the catch on the window, but her fingers, greasy with sweat, slid off. She tried again.

"Cally." Jules's voice, calm and even. Then there she was, standing in the living room doorway.

"I've called the police," Cally said and hated how meek her voice sounded.

Jules looked wounded. She touched her hand to her chest. "I just want to talk."

"You just let yourself into my *house*."

Jules waved a hand in front of her. "Well, you live here, but technically it's my house. My money paid for it. It's unreasonable of you not to expect me to have a key."

Now Cally was angry. "I earned every penny of that money. It was *my* inheritance from my parents that paid for this house. Not *you*."

"And whose money did you live on all these years that meant you didn't have to *touch* that inheritance? Mine. We aren't divorced yet. That makes this house half mine. I let you buy it to give you time, to give you space to release how ridiculous you're being." Jules took a deep breath. "Cally, I'm here because I'm worried about you." Jules took a step into the room. "We all are, all the people who care about you." Another step.

Cally countered it with a step back, and her knees touched the sofa. Jules had her hand in her pocket. Cally could see she was holding something.

"In the beginning, I wondered if you were having some kind of breakdown. And I was angry with you—and hurt. I couldn't understand why you were throwing everything we had down the toilet. Then I realised." Jules took another step, and now she was in the room and completely blocking the doorway.

Cally looked around the room for something—anything—she could use to defend herself. A scented candle and a novel on the small table to her left. Great.

"I realised someone must be making you do this. I keep seeing the same man coming and going from here at all hours," Jules said.

"Man? What man?" Mixed in with the confusion, Cally felt the old dread and fear surge to the surface. This was how it had been when they were together, when Jules ruled her. Then, she heard the other part of what Jules said. "How do you know who comes and goes? Oh my God, have you been *watching* me?"

Jules tutted. "You make it sound so creepy. I'm your wife, Cally, whether you want to acknowledge that or not. I said on our wedding day I'd always watch over you, and I meant it. Even when I couldn't do it myself, I've always had eyes on you, Cally."

"Jesus fucking Christ," Cally said in a whisper. All the air felt like it'd left her lungs. "You're crazy. All those years together and I just thought you were horrible. But you're actually a complete lunatic."

Jules frowned. "That's a mean thing to say. But you always were ungrateful. Nothing I did for you was ever enough." She stepped closer again, and Cally could see she now had hold of whatever it was in her coat pocket.

Cally decided she was out of time. She said a quick prayer, turned, shoved the sash window up as hard as she could, and threw herself out like she was in an action movie. She landed head first in the hedge that lined her front wall—better than head first into the wall itself. She jumped up—didn't dare look behind her—and ran.

CHAPTER FIFTEEN

Now

Cally didn't dare look behind her. She ran as fast as she could—and she knew she could run fast. All those miles she clocked up in the woods needed to count for something now. She ran and ran and prayed a car would come along. She even wished Laurie would come back. Cally strained her ears trying to hear if there was someone behind her. All she could hear was her own blood beating and the slap of her feet on the wet ground.

She barely heard the sound of the engine as it came up behind her. At the last minute she turned and nearly cried with relief.

Laurie slowed to a stop beside her and rolled down the window. "What's going on?"

Cally couldn't catch her breath. "Behind me. Someone. Orange jacket. Chasing. Shit."

"Someone was chasing you?" Laurie asked.

Cally nodded and pulled open the passenger door of the truck. She climbed in. "Drive."

Cally could have kissed her when, instead of asking a bunch of annoying questions, Laurie hit the door lock button and accelerated down the road.

"I'm going to let you catch your breath and then you can tell me what on earth is going on."

Cally nodded. "Thanks." And then after a moment. "Turn around."

"Pardon?" Laurie asked.

"Turn around. I want to see if the little orange fucker is still there," Cally said.

"I'm sorry. I see you running like a bat out of hell, and you tell me you're being chased. Instead of driving to the nearest police station, you want to go back and see if we can kick off a bit of round two?"

"Please. We're safe in your truck. The doors are locked. Besides, I'm not sure…"

"Not sure what?" Laurie asked.

"I don't know. Can we just go back, please?"

Laurie sighed like a much put-upon woman, which Cally guessed she was. "Fine. But this is the exact opposite thing they tell you to do."

"What are you talking about? What *who* tell you to do?"

"Movies. Crime documentaries."

Cally stopped listening. She was scanning the roadside for a flash of orange. Something caught her eye, and she turned her head to look. She ducked her head to see out the back window. Then her eyes went down to the back seat. All the air went out of her, and she went lightheaded.

"What's that?" she asked Laurie. To her own ears she sounded winded.

"What's what?" Laurie asked. She'd begun scanning the road as well.

"In the back seat."

Laurie glanced into the back seat. "What? My hi-vis jacket?"

"It's orange."

"So?"

"Stop the truck," Cally said, and her hand was already on the door handle.

"We're back here again, are we?" Laurie asked. She slowed the truck to a stop and pressed the door lock button. "There you go. Unlocked. You're free to leave."

Cally paused. Was she being totally paranoid? She glanced in the back seat again. The jacket looked dry. Jesus, was she totally losing her mind?

"Lock the doors," Cally said.

"Are you sure? Because it kind of sounded like you think it was me chasing you up the road," Laurie said, angry now.

"I'm sorry. I just saw the jacket and—"

"And thought I'd chased you down wearing that, then got back in my truck to come and find you?"

"Why *did* you come and find me?" asked Cally, wary again now.

Laurie sighed and scrubbed her face with her hands. "Because I'm a glutton for punishment?" She looked at Cally with cool eyes. "I felt bad. I drove away, and it started pissing down with rain. I know how these roads can get. And I know I blindsided you again when I told you we might try to fight your planning permission. I didn't think it was right to just leave you."

Cally nodded and looked out the windscreen. She scanned both sides of the road.

"Cally? What the fuck is going on?" Laurie asked, the anger gone now. Now, she just sounded bewildered, and Cally couldn't blame her. She must seem like a madwoman.

"I saw someone in orange when I was walking. I didn't think much of it the first time, and then it kept appearing. And then someone stepped out of the forest."

"And threatened you?"

"No. They ran towards me."

"Okay."

"So, I ran."

"Right."

"I know how I sound." Cally turned to face Laurie, expecting to see wariness and that superior smirk. Instead Laurie looked…gentle. "You think I've lost it."

"No. I don't. If you say someone chased you—"

"I'm not entirely sure they chased me."

"You must have reason to think they did if you say they did."

"I don't know any more." Suddenly, Cally felt very tired. "Can you please just take me home?"

"Cally—"

"*Please*, Laurie. Take me home."

Laurie sighed. "You can't tell me someone's chasing you, accuse *me*, and then decide it's all fine, you never got chased, and now you want to go home."

"I know. I know I must seem like a nutcase. But please, Laurie. Just take me home. I want to go home."

"Fine. Okay. Sure."

Cally could feel Laurie's eyes bore into her for a moment with all the things she wanted to say, but she didn't ask any more questions. She put the truck into gear and drove Cally home. Cally leaned back in her seat and shut her eyes.

CHAPTER SIXTEEN

Laurie pulled up outside the house, and here they were again. Cally was drained. She looked at her house and thought she'd give anything to sink into a hot bath in her nasty green bathroom. The last twenty-four hours had been too much. She questioned now whether she had been chased at all, whether anybody had been chasing her, or if her bruised and battered brain was trying to conjure up a new monster now the real one was dead. A monster in an orange jacket, just like Jules had been on that last day.

She sighed. She was grateful to Laurie, but right now she just wanted her to leave. She didn't want to answer any questions or explain what the fuck happened back there. But she guessed she owed Laurie some kind of explanation. Even if it was just to keep her from going into the village and telling everyone Cally was insane.

"Do you want to come inside?" Cally asked.

Laurie shook her head and smiled. It was gentle and kind, and Cally almost began to cry. "No, I won't come in, not today. Look, there's clearly stuff going on with you, and I would like to know what it is, but you don't owe me anything. And you're tired. How about we pick this up tomorrow? I could make dinner? Then, you can tell me whatever you want to…or not."

Cally nodded. She wasn't used to kindness. Hadn't had it for years. Laurie wasn't pushing, and it felt alien and lovely and reminded Cally of how things used to be before Jules, when she expected—and often got—kindness. Cally believed her when she said she wouldn't ask Cally to talk about anything she didn't want to.

"I meant what I said yesterday," Laurie said. "I want to be your friend."

"And friends eat dinner," Cally said and smiled. It was an effort—she was so tired—but she managed a small one.

"Oh yes," Laurie said, catching on that Cally wanted to lighten the mood. "Sometimes together."

Cally laughed. "Oh yeah?"

Laurie nodded solemnly. "And drink wine."

"You don't say?"

"And chat."

"About the weather?" Cally asked.

"About all sorts of things. TV shows, films. Sport."

Cally wrinkled her nose and shook her head. "I don't talk about sport."

"Okay, well maybe I'll keep that for my other friends."

"I think it's for the best."

Laurie reached for a notepad and pen on her dashboard. "Shall we say seven? Here." Laurie tore off a sheet and handed it to Cally. "My address."

"Thanks." Cally took the note.

"Oh wait, your car."

Cally waved her hand. "Don't worry. I'll sort it." Not that she was sure how to go about that.

"Do you need your car before tomorrow night?" Laurie asked.

Cally thought. She had the builders coming tomorrow and hadn't planned on leaving Five Oaks. "No, I don't think I need my car."

"Okay, cool. I'll pick you up just before seven. We can go and get your car, and you can follow me to my place," Laurie said.

"Are you sure?" Cally asked. It would certainly help her out.

"Yeah. As long as you promise not to make me stop, get out, and storm off in the middle of a country road again," Laurie said.

Cally shot her a look. "I don't think we need to revisit the conversation before the big storm-off just yet, do we?"

Laurie's mouth snapped shut. "No. Probably not."

"Good. Look, I'm going to go. I'm dead on my feet and I want a bath and a nap."

"Understood," Laurie said. "See you tomorrow."

Cally nodded and got out of the truck. She looked back once and waved at Laurie as she drove away. The rain had created huge puddles all over the drive, and Laurie splashed mud all over her truck on the way out.

CHAPTER SEVENTEEN

Cally woke to bright, cold winter sun streaming through her bedroom window. She smiled and hit the off button on her alarm and checked her weather app. Six degrees, so bloody freezing, but in winter you took what you could get. And she would take the cold with the sun if it meant not traipsing around waterlogged fields with builders, getting soaked with rain and battered by icy winds.

Cally had been here five months now, but she still wasn't used to the colder temperatures. Not that it didn't get cold in London, but up here everything was harsher somehow.

She contemplated going for a run. It was the perfect morning for it, but she had so much to do before the builders showed up. They were going through the architect's plans today and drawing up a schedule for the works. For the first time in weeks, Cally was going to look at the old cabins, except this time, she was so much closer to making them look like the images that had been in her head for so long. It also meant if Laurie and her forest people did challenge the planning, they could at least start on the existing cabins and pitches while they waited for the outcome.

The builders were due at nine, which gave her an hour and a half to get ready and to run through her notes and list of questions before she met with them.

There was a knock at the door, and Cally was pleased to see the builders were on time. That boded well for the huge amount of money she was pouring into their work.

The builders, Phil and Joe, wanted to walk to the fields where

Cally planned to put the pitches first. Phil glanced around the field and then at the plans. "Yeah, this will work really well. A lot to clear, though, before we can start the groundwork."

Cally nodded. The field had been left to itself for so long that it was badly overgrown. Rubbish fluttered in the wind and caught on brambles and hedges and whatever else made up the tangled mess. There was an earthy, fecund smell that Cally sort of liked.

They walked on, heading into the next field where Cally was planning the first section of caravan pitches. It was in the same state as the first field and would need a lot of work to clear as well.

The sun had stayed with them, and even though the wind bit, Cally was enjoying herself. Last night after she got home, she'd had a bath and read a book and tried to relax, but the tension was still there. All the memories pushed against each other in her head, trying to get out.

This morning, she woke up and all of it was gone. Maybe it was the weather and the prospect of today, which she'd been waiting so long for. She tried not to think about what Laurie said yesterday. A judicial review was hard to get and expensive. Hopefully, at Laurie's meeting today, they would decide it just wasn't worth it. She hadn't said anything to the builders yet because she didn't want them getting spooked and backing out of the job.

Cally realised her mind had wandered when she saw Joe looking at her expectantly. "Sorry, what?"

"I said, shall we go and see the cabins now?"

"Yes, of course," Cally said. This was the bit she'd been waiting for. The cabins took up most of her thoughts about Five Oaks, and she couldn't wait to see all her dreams and planning finally realised.

As they reached the wood Five Oaks was named for, a grey cloud moved across the sun. The view was still beautiful, though. Her property was surrounded by the forest, and she guessed her wood had been part of it, once upon a time. It was only a few acres, but in spring it was full of bluebells, and in summer the ancient oaks and beech trees offered shades of green that took your breath away. It was Cally's favourite part of the property.

The cabins were nestled in amongst the trees. The architect she'd used was clever and had managed to fit in more cabins without losing a single healthy tree, which was one of the stipulations Cally had made. This wood was what made her fall in love with the property, and she refused to lose any part of it. It had been here longer than four generations of her family, and it would probably outlast another four.

"They're structurally sound, aren't they?" Phil asked her.

"Yes, I had a survey done. Bit mouldy and damp but safe."

"Okay, let's check out the first one," Phil said.

Cally took out a huge ring of keys and found the right one. The door squealed as she pushed it open, and the smell of mildew was almost overpowering when they stepped inside.

"Wow. That's pretty bad," Cally said and heard the sound of a cash register ringing loudly in her ears.

Phil sucked in a breath, which definitely meant he was about to say something that would cost her money. "Doesn't smell watertight to me. Or feel it." Phil stamped on the soggy floor to demonstrate.

Cally hated to admit it didn't to her either. Which was strange because the survey had said all the cabins were basically okay, and mainly cosmetic work needed to be done.

They approached the bathroom, and the smell was stronger here. Cally pushed open the door. The whole room was a flooded mess. "Jesus," Joe said and immediately went to the source of the leaking water. Someone had detached the pipe that connected the sink to water. He quickly did it back up and tightened it as best as he could.

"How did that happen?" Cally asked. The look that passed between Phil and Joe didn't escape her.

"Looks like someone might have been messing around in here," Phil said.

They quickly checked the other rooms—they remained undisturbed. Small mercies, Cally thought.

"Why would someone do that?" she asked.

Phil shrugged. "Could be bored kids. Out in the middle of nowhere they get bored and sometimes destructive."

"But I have the keys. How did they get in?"

Phil shrugged again, not very interested in the answer to that one. "Unlocked window?" he offered. "We should go around and check the rest."

Cally guessed they should. She could ponder the conundrum of the locked door later.

Down to the last cabin and the so far, so good. Apart from the first one, the others were exactly as she'd seen them before.

The last cabin was furthest back in the woods and slightly away from the others. Cally could see something was wrong as soon as they walked into the clearing.

"Oh shit," she said.

"Door's open," Joe said, helpfully stating the obvious.

The door was wide open, as though whoever opened it didn't much care if Cally knew they'd been inside. As they got closer, Cally could see it had been forced open. The wood on the frame and by the lock was splintered and gouged.

"Fucking hell," Cally said. She rubbed her face with both hands and braced herself for what they'd find inside.

"Me and Joe can go in by ourselves if you like," Phil offered.

Part of Cally wanted to take him up on it, but a bigger part wanted to go in and see for herself instead of waiting outside like some scared little wallflower. "Thanks, but I'll come."

Phil nodded. He was about to speak when something inside the cabin growled.

Chapter Eighteen

"What was that?" Joe asked.

"Sounds like an animal," Phil said.

Cally was torn between running away and going inside to see what damage had been caused in this cabin. She took a step closer to the doorway and tried to peer inside. All she could see was the hall, which looked pretty undisturbed apart from the dirty floor. Mud had been tracked in and out with no concern for the rug. Some looked like animal tracks.

The growl came again, and Cally took another step closer. Something was standing at the end of the hall. She could just about make out its shape in the dingy light.

It looked like a dog. Cally took another step forward, so now she was standing in the doorway. The dog stepped back and hit the bookcase behind it. Its back hunched, and it bared its teeth at Cally.

"I guess it wandered in there," Cally said.

"Yeah. Stray," Phil said from behind her.

Cally wondered if it was the stray from the other night. Probably. "What should we do, then? Wait for it to come back out?" Cally asked.

"That sounds best. I'd rather not get bitten," Phil said.

Cally looked at the dog again, who whined and dipped its head. She felt sorry for the creature. She couldn't tell for sure with the poor light, but it looked emaciated. And scared. So scared.

"Hey," she said softly. "It's okay."

The dog whined again and dropped its head. Behind her, Phil or Joe moved, and the dog's head came back up. It bared its teeth and growled, low and dangerous.

"The question is, who's broken in?" Joe said. "Looks like they've taken a crowbar to the door."

"Probably someone needing a place to sleep for the night," Phil said. "Or kids. Before Cally bought the place, it was empty for months. I'd like to get in and see what damage we need to put right, but maybe when the dog's gone."

Cally agreed. They walked back to the house. Cally was mentally going through the contents of her fridge to see what she could bring back for the dog. She couldn't stop thinking about it. It must be so hungry and cold and scared.

"Do you think it'll go?" Cally asked. "The dog?"

Phil shrugged. "Probably only went in because the door was open. Depending on how long, might have made a little den in there. Now it's seen us, it'll probably clear off. If not, call out the council. They'll send the dog warden out to pick it up. I can call if you want."

"No, that's okay. I can sort it. I'll walk back up to the cabin later to see if it's gone. I can take photos inside and send them to you to save you coming back up."

Phil nodded.

Cally wasn't sure she wanted the dog to clear off. Which was strange because she'd never had a pet, not even growing up. Jules hadn't liked animals at all, so they'd never discussed a pet.

Cally remembered what the dog looked like in the cabin, scared and cornered.

When the builders left with a plan to email Cally the schedule of works they'd agreed and a start date, she walked into the house. Christ, it was bloody freezing again. Cally went straight to the thermostat and saw it was back down to the lowest temperature. She'd really have to get someone out to look at it. There was no reason for the dial to keep turning itself down like that. Admittedly, she didn't know anything about electrics. Probably there was some cataclysmic fault that would cost a fortune to repair. And she would pay it because she *hated* the cold.

In the kitchen, Cally found half a kilo of minced beef in the fridge. She didn't remember taking it out of the freezer, but then she also couldn't remember the last time she'd made a meal for herself—it had been a busy couple of days. She sniffed the mince, decided it smelled okay, and set it on the hob to fry it off. Cally didn't know if you could give dogs raw mince, but she didn't want to take a chance.

Cally got a bottle of water out of the cupboard and found a plastic container that would work as a water bowl. What about towels and blankets? If the dog was living in the cabin, it couldn't be very warm—did dogs get cold? Maybe it would appreciate something soft to lie on.

Cally stopped. What the fuck was she doing? Was she trying to befriend a stray and apparently unfriendly dog? No, of course not, she told herself. She felt sorry for it, that was all. Something about the sight of it cowering in the cold, unloved and discarded. She was a soft touch, that was all. She definitely didn't want to befriend the bloody thing. So then why did she stop Phil calling the dog warden?

Cally didn't want to think about that question. She tipped the mince into some Tupperware, grabbed the water and container, and went into the utility room to look for an old towel or blanket.

CHAPTER NINETEEN

By the time Cally got back up to the cabin, the rain had really started to come down. The clouds were low and grey, and she could hardly believe it had been so pretty out earlier. That was the British weather for you, though, and even more so up here in Gloucestershire.

The door was wide open as they left it, and Cally strained her ears for any sign of the dog. Satisfied there were no low growls or whines, she carefully stepped inside.

The cabin's hallway ran up the middle with the rooms branching off to the left and right. On the left were the bathroom, kitchen, and then bedroom, and on the right was the living room.

Cally took a quick look in the bathroom and was relieved when everything looked okay. The kitchen was fine too, so that left the bedroom and living room. She went right, into the living room, and saw immediately that this was where the dog had been staying.

The previous owners had removed most of the furniture to sell, so the room was empty. On the floor were a collection of small bones, leaves that had blown in, and lots of muddy doggy footprints. No dog, though.

The bedroom was a different story altogether. Something human had been staying in here. Any bedding they'd used was gone, but empty crisp bags and sandwich packets, drinks cans and bottles littered the floor. On the wall in black spray paint were a huge and crudely drawn pair of eyes. It covered almost the whole wall. Cally took an involuntary step back.

What the hell was that about? Her? She looked around the floor again. If it was kids who'd been using the cabin, wouldn't you expect to find old condoms, lager cans, cigarette butts? There was none of that here.

Didn't mean the eyes were about her, though. How could they be? All the same, she was unnerved. Someone who drew that had been living in her cabin, metres from her house. And not that long ago, judging by the detritus on the floor. None of it looked old or faded.

Cally thought again about the figure in orange. Maybe that hadn't been in her head. But if that *had* been real, and if the drawing on the wall was about *her*, who was it? The only person Cally could think of who would do something like this was Jules. And Jules was dead.

Wasn't she? They hadn't found her body yet, but there was irrefutable proof she'd died. Wasn't there?

No, Cally didn't want to go down that road because *that* road led to madness. Jules was dead, she'd imagined the figure in orange, and this was some poor person with mental health problems who'd decided to stay in her cabin for a while. That was *all*.

Satisfied she'd steered herself safely back to sanity, Cally went about putting the food and water down for the dog and trying to fashion some sort of bed for it in the living room out the towels and blanket she'd brought.

She hoped the dog would come back. She remembered how it looked in the hallway and hoped the food would please it. One small good thing in a life that so far seemed to be a very hard and very lonely one.

Cally decided she'd be back tomorrow. She'd go into town and buy the dog some more suitable food. And then, what, befriend it? Did she even want a dog? She wasn't entirely sure what she was doing, or why she didn't just call the warden. It was a feeling she couldn't explain or really even understand. An idea that she *needed* to help this dog.

Cally sighed. She had no idea what she was doing. A sensible person would call the warden. The dog was probably riddled with fleas and ticks and worms and God knew what else. Did she really think a blanket and a bit of minced beef was helping it? What was the point?

Unless the point was to get the dog to trust her. Why would she want that, though? It wasn't like she was planning on keeping it or anything. Cally had enough going on at the moment without adding a pet to the mix. Feeding it today was fine, but tomorrow, she'd call the warden. It was the sensible thing to do.

She took one last look around the living room, satisfied that when the dog came back, it would be able to see the food, water, and cosy bed Cally set up.

On the way out of the cabin, she found a decent-sized rock and propped it in front of the door. It wouldn't do for the wind to blow the door shut because then how would the dog get back in?

She walked back to the house. Her pocket vibrated with a text or email, and she pulled her mobile out to look. Sian. Cally hadn't heard from her since yesterday and wondered if she was embarrassed about getting so drunk. She needn't be because Cally had been just as pissed. Cally had held off messaging her, not wanting to make Sian feel awkward. She shouldn't have worried because Sian wanted to know what Cally was up to Saturday night. Apparently there was a comedy night in the next town over, and Sian wanted to go.

Cally texted back that she'd love to before she could think about it and talk herself out of it. She was kind of enjoying having a bit of a social life. The last three years had been pretty dry except for Jules's work things and dinners in swanky places with people Jules called friends but privately bitched about to Cally all the time.

Cally tried to remember what it was like to have friends.

Before Jules she hadn't exactly been inundated, but she'd believed she had a small group of good friends, and she'd seen them regularly. When Jules came along, that stopped. Cally didn't exactly blame her friends for disappearing. She knew how it looked. Jules made things difficult. Difficult for Cally when she saw them, texting and calling all the time, or booking dinners and shows and plays on the same days, so Cally always had to cut the catch-ups short, which made it look like Cally didn't have time for them, didn't want to see them.

And Cally admitted to herself she'd been too weak to push back against Jules—not that she realised what was happening at first. But after a while she did know Jules's behaviour was deliberate, intentional. When her friends started forgetting to invite her to things or always seemed too busy to meet up, Cally knew then. They didn't like Jules, and they'd had enough of Cally.

One friend tried to tell her in the early days, tried to warn Cally that Jules's behaviour wasn't normal, wasn't okay. Cally didn't want to hear it. She was *in love* with Jules, wasn't she? Cally was ashamed of her response to her friend's genuine concern. She'd called her jealous. Said she—the group—liked the fact Cally was perennially single, always available to listen to them moan about their partners. Always available to be a plus-one to their events when they were single. Now Cally had someone, and they didn't like it. She'd honestly believed it as well. Even when her friend shook her head sadly and tried to show Cally something she'd printed off the internet—seven signs you're in a controlling relationship, or something like that.

So, all her friends had drifted away until she was alone.

Now things were looking up. She had two people who she wouldn't exactly call friends, but with some cultivation, they could be. The thought made her happy. It made her feel less lonely. Not that she felt the same way about Laurie as she did about Sian. Sian was purely *like*, and Laurie was something much more complicated.

Cally didn't want to dwell on that, though. Laurie'd offered friendship, and Cally needed that much more than she needed a relationship. She didn't know if she would ever be ready for another one of those. Logically, she knew not everyone was like Jules. But when she thought about being with someone else, she got a sick feeling in her stomach and fluttery in her chest. Laurie was good-looking and Cally wasn't deluded, she could admit she was attracted to her, but for now that was as far as she was willing to go. Besides, Laurie wasn't pummelling Cally with declarations of love. She'd clearly said she wanted to be friends. Even if Cally was contemplating the idea of more—not that she was—Laurie wasn't offering it.

Cally's phone pinged again, and she smiled when she saw Sian's champagne and party hat emoji. One other thing she knew—she wasn't getting drunk like she had Saturday night. She was staying sober. And she was driving home.

Chapter Twenty

Cally put the back on her earring and looked at herself in the mirror. She'd do. She wasn't sure why she was so bothered with what she looked like, anyway. It was only dinner at Laurie's. Ever since she'd admitted to herself she liked Laurie in a way she didn't like Sian, she'd been feeling funny about tonight.

It very clearly was not a date. She didn't *want* it to be a date. She wasn't ready, plus Laurie was actively trying to sabotage her business, so she wasn't really sure why she was giving her the time of day.

Cally briefly remembered the drawing on the wall. She couldn't get those dripping black eyes out of her mind. She remembered what Jules said to her on that last day. About watching Cally, about having *eyes* on her. But that and this were not connected. They couldn't be.

The doorbell rang downstairs, and Cally guessed it must be Laurie, come to pick her up. Something fluttered briefly in her stomach before she pushed it away with annoyance. She went downstairs.

"Hello," Laurie said when Cally opened the door. "For you." She thrust out a bunch of flowers. And not just any flowers, wildflowers that looked as if Laurie picked them herself.

"Yes, I did pick them, and no I didn't get them from the forest," Laurie said, and Cally noticed she'd gone a little red in the face.

"They're beautiful. Where did you get them?" Cally asked. She went back into the house, and Laurie followed her into the kitchen.

"I grow them," Laurie said.

"I should have guessed you were a gardener," Cally said and found a vase for the flowers. She put them on the kitchen table.

"Garden, bake, cook, and go for long walks in nature."

"What a catch," Cally said and laughed. "So am I to assume that you've prepared us a three course restaurant-quality meal?"

"But of course," Laurie said and, joking, held out her arm for Cally. Cally played along and slipped her arm inside Laurie's. They walked to the front door. "Your carriage awaits." Laurie motioned to her truck—sparkling clean, Cally noticed. Did she do that especially for Cally?

"Wow, it's black. And there I was, thinking you drove a mud-brown truck," Cally said.

"Ha ha. It's your drive that makes it so dirty," Laurie said.

They picked up Cally's car from the village, and Cally was glad to have it back. She followed Laurie down various winding, unlit country roads, with one eye on Laurie's tail lights. She kept the other on the forest flanking her for sight of the figure in orange.

It was stupid. The more time that passed, the more she believed she'd, if not imagined it, then certainly misinterpreted it—embellished it, perhaps. She would talk to Laurie about it tonight. It was embarrassing, but likely Laurie would help put her mind at rest. Same with the eyes in her cabin. Laurie was from here, born and bred. She'd probably even have some idea of who'd done it.

Laurie flicked on her indicator and turned left onto a short driveway. She parked to the side so Cally could pull up alongside her. A security light clicked on, and Cally could see Laurie had been telling the truth when she said she was a gardener. The front garden was filled with plants and shrubs, which Cally knew would look beautiful in spring and summer. Several large trees flanked the edges of Laurie's property.

Cally got out of her car and joined Laurie by the front door. "It's beautiful," she said, indicating the front garden.

"Thanks. It was a lot of work, but I've got it where I want it now. You'll have to come in spring when it really comes alive," Laurie said.

"I'd love to. I'll probably steal some of your ideas for my drive while I'm here," Cally said.

"No problem. I can help you design it if you want," Laurie said and unlocked the front door.

Inside, Cally was hit with the smell of fresh bread and cooking stew. Her stomach growled loudly, and Laurie laughed. "Hungry?"

"Starving. Did you actually make bread?" Cally asked, following Laurie into the kitchen.

"I did. I told you, I'm a baker."

"I thought you meant cakes," Cally said.

"Them too. Here, sit down."

Cally took a seat at the dining table and looked around. Laurie's kitchen was filled with bottles and jars, cookbooks and utensils, pots and pans. It was a proper cook's kitchen, and Cally wondered if Laurie had underplayed her abilities in the kitchen.

Cally watched as Laurie lifted the lid on the slow cooker, sprinkled something in it, stirred, then put the lid back on.

"Shouldn't be much longer now," Laurie said. "You want a tour of the house?"

"Sure," Cally said.

"I'd show you the back garden, but it's too dark to see anything. Plus everything's pretty much died back, so it doesn't look that great."

Cally followed Laurie into her living room. Two big overstuffed sofas faced a TV almost as big as Cally's car. Bookshelves lined the walls and were crammed with books on every subject imaginable. Cally ignored the sick feeling in her stomach when she saw Jules's memoirs up on the shelf.

It didn't mean anything. Loads of people had bought that book.

Upstairs were three bedrooms. Laurie clearly used one as an office and another as a spare bedroom. When Cally walked into Laurie's bedroom, she felt herself blush a little and told herself not to be stupid. Laurie was giving her a tour of the house, not trying to seduce Cally.

All the same, Cally looked at the bed, neatly made with a bright blue bedspread, and thought it looked comfortable. She found herself wondering how many times the headboard had rattled up here.

The blush caught fire, and to her mortification, Cally knew she'd turned bright red.

Laurie cleared her throat and hid a smile. "Shall we go back downstairs? I'll pour you some wine."

"Just one glass," Cally said. "I'm definitely driving home later. Don't want you having to buy more tyres."

Laurie laughed. “Good. Although you moved whatever it was in the drive that punctured them.”

Except Cally hadn’t. In all honesty, she’d forgotten Laurie said she’d driven over something.

Chapter Twenty-one

Cally put down her knife and fork and leaned back in her chair. "That was incredible."

Laurie grinned. "Yeah? Glad you liked it."

"It was the best meal I've eaten in ages. And the bread…" Cally sighed and rolled her eyes.

"Well, I'm glad I got your seal of approval. It's nice to have someone to cook for. Gets boring when it's just you."

"I know what you mean. Well, I'm up for eating your food any time," Cally said.

"Noted," Laurie said and started clearing the plates.

"Let me help." Cally stood.

"No, no. Please, sit down. Drink some more wine and tell me again how much you liked my food."

Cally laughed. "I didn't realise you were so needy."

"You have no idea." Laurie looked at Cally and waggled her eyebrows.

Cally burst out laughing and she felt a flush creep up her neck at the double meaning. "What's for dessert?" she asked.

"Crème brûlée because you're posh and I wanted more compliments," Laurie said.

Cally sat back and watched Laurie work. She admired the way she effortlessly mixed and measured and poured. Cally found her eyes drifting to Laurie's butt when she bent over the oven. Nice.

She caught herself. *Nice*? What was she doing? Ogling Laurie like some dirty old man. Laurie, who'd given no sign she was interested in

Cally like that, and even if she had been, Cally was in no position to take her up on it.

"Everything okay?" Laurie asked. "You've got a funny look on your face."

"I'm okay, just thinking," Cally said and leaned back in her chair in an effort to put some distance between them when Laurie came to sit down.

"Oh yeah? Want to share?" Laurie asked, not seeming to notice the way Cally leaned away from her. "Is it about yesterday?"

"Yes," Cally lied—sort of lied. It had been on her mind.

Laurie nodded. "I'm not sure what happened. I am sorry, though, for my part in it."

"You didn't do anything," Cally said.

"I shouldn't have left you to walk in the rain like that," Laurie said.

"It was my choice. I made you stop the truck."

Laurie nodded. "I suppose. So, what happened?"

Cally took a deep breath and wondered how much she should trust Laurie with. Laurie, who'd she'd only known a couple of days and who she'd hated at first. "Well, now I'm not sure *anything* happened. At the time I thought…"

"You said you thought someone was chasing you," Laurie said.

Cally nodded. "Yes. Yes, that's what I thought."

"Maybe someone *was* chasing you," Laurie said. "It happens, right?"

"Have you ever heard of anything around here like that?" Cally felt stupid saying the words, but Laurie regarded her seriously without any hint she thought Cally was mad or paranoid. It gave her the courage to continue. "Or why someone would be wearing bright orange? A local running club or something?"

"There's no local running club that I can think of who wears orange. But some runners wear bright colours in the forest for safety. I have an orange hi-vis jacket."

"So, that could be what it was," Cally said.

"What exactly happened, though? Presumably you don't just randomly assume someone's chasing you for no reason."

"While I was walking, I kept seeing this flash of orange out of the corner of my eye. I eventually stopped to see who was there, and this person stepped out of the forest and just kind of *stood* there and looked at me."

"Looked at you? Like…angry?" Laurie asked.

"I don't know. They had their hood up."

"Well, that's fucking creepy," Laurie said.

Cally was relieved Laurie thought so too. "Then I ran."

"And they chased you?" Laurie asked.

Cally thought back. "I'm not sure. I mean…"

"You didn't stop to check. Why would you? I wouldn't."

Relieved, Cally continued, "Exactly. I just ran. When I stopped, I couldn't see them."

"So maybe they didn't chase you?" Laurie suggested.

"Maybe not," Cally admitted.

"Still a bloody weird thing to do. I'm glad I came to my senses and drove back. It's possible the truck scared them off," Laurie said.

For a moment, Cally thought it really was convenient Laurie turned back when she did.

Laurie, who had an orange jacket in her car.

Cally felt guilty for thinking it, but she couldn't help it. Jules taught her all about how people weren't who you thought they were. Jules, who'd chased Cally wearing an orange jacket.

Maybe that's what it was. Cally was still being haunted by Jules and all the fucked-up shit she'd done. Everyone who owned an orange jacket was a potential threat now. Even charming gardeners who baked their own bread. Laurie had given Cally no reason not to trust her.

Laurie, who she'd known for only a few days.

"There's something else. You're from here, so you might know the answer," Cally said.

"Go for it."

"I inspected the cabins today with the builders. The ones I'm renovating?"

Laurie nodded for her to go on.

"Well, in one of them, someone had got in and vandalised a water pipe. The whole place was flooded."

"Oh, Cally, that's shit. I'm sorry." Laurie sounded genuinely upset for her.

"It's fine, the whole thing is being redone anyway. But in another cabin, well, someone had clearly been staying in there."

"Like squatting?"

"I suppose that's what you'd call it. It didn't seem like kids, though. No beer cans or…other things."

Laurie grinned.

Cally continued, "But they'd spray-painted a massive pair of eyes on the bedroom wall."

The grin dropped of Laurie's face. "What?"

"You think it's weird too?" Cally asked.

"Weird? It's fucking stalkerish when you put it alongside the person following you the other day. Was there anything else on the wall? Like, tags or something?"

Cally shook her head. "No, just the eyes."

"So, someone's squatting in your cabin drawing eyes on the wall and maybe following you," Laurie said.

"Yes, that's about the long and short of it," Cally said. "Except, I don't *know* someone's following me, and the eyes on the wall could mean nothing."

"I guess. Have you noticed anything else?" Laurie asked.

"No. Except…" Cally wasn't sure how much to say.

"Except what?"

Cally sighed then wagged a finger at Laurie. "This goes no further."

"Okay."

"I mean it."

"*Okay.* It won't go any further."

"I've been getting these letters. For a while now, they aren't new. And they're still addressed to my old house."

"What letters?"

"Malicious ones. Never threatening but…unpleasant," Cally said. "I've been getting them since my wife killed herself."

Chapter Twenty-two

They'd moved into Laurie's living room, and she'd started a fire in the wood burner. It was cosy with the lights down, and the sofas were as comfy as they looked.

Cally wasn't sure when she'd decided to tell Laurie the whole story. She barely knew her, after all, but she needed to tell someone. And why not Laurie?

"My wife—Jules—died nine months ago. Do you know Beachy Head?" Cally asked.

Laurie nodded. "Cliffs on the south coast."

"Right. She jumped off. You probably heard about it. My wife was Jules Kay. But you might already know that," Cally said.

Laurie looked uncomfortable, and Cally wondered if she had been a fan. So many had been. Not that she blamed them, Jules had been successful for a reason. She'd started as a stand-up comic and parlayed her career into panel shows and presenting and documentaries. People loved her because she was talented."

"I knew who Jules Kay was. And I'd heard you were her wife before you came up here. People were excited we were getting a celebrity," Laurie asked.

Cally laughed. "I'm not sure I count as one of those. I tried to stay out of it as much as possible. Then she killed herself, and I was splashed across the news."

"I did hear about that. You couldn't really get away from it for a while there. She was very popular," Laurie said.

Cally nodded. "Most of the country heard about it. She was a national treasure apparently."

Laurie nodded, her mouth a grim line. "I heard she also broke into your house and tried to attack you. That some people didn't believe you."

Cally nodded. "Yes, she did do that. I got away, though. And then, the story goes, she realised she was going to be exposed for who she really was and decided to jump off a cliff rather than face up to it. And yes, some people think I lied. Think I wanted her money and wanted a divorce. That there was a prenuptial agreement and if I divorced her there would be no money for me. There's huge threads and websites online dedicated to my Machiavellian ways."

"I'll be honest, I don't read all that gossip stuff. I heard she broke into your house, and the police were looking for her. I heard she killed herself. I assume there's some kind of backstory to her behaviour, that there was a reason you left her. That this sort of thing wasn't out of character for her."

Laurie had guessed, then, that Jules wasn't the saint she appeared to be. It was a relief and also humiliating to feel so exposed to someone who was basically a stranger.

Cally shook her head. "No, it wasn't out of character. It had been building for a while. She told me, on that last day—she said she had eyes on me and that she'd been watching me for a long time. When I saw those eyes in the cabin…"

Laurie reached across the sofas and took Cally's hands. "Yeah, that must have brought it back. Especially after being chased."

Cally was relieved Laurie understood.

"What about the letters?" Laurie asked.

"They started coming after Jules died."

"What do they say?"

"Nasty stuff. Stuff about how I was responsible for Jules's death. How I rode on her coat-tails and married her because I was fame hungry—which was ridiculous because I hated all that stuff."

"Do they ever threaten you?" Laurie asked.

"Not overtly. They say they wish it had been me that went over the cliff. That it should have been me."

"Did you go to the police?" Laurie asked.

Cally shook her head. "No. I give them to my solicitor, who keeps them in case anything else happens or they get worse. So far, nothing has ever happened. Whoever's sending them never went to my home and they had my address. It's probably just some saddo sitting in their bedroom."

"Cally, you need to go to the police," Laurie said. "Especially now, after what's happened."

"What *has* happened, Laurie? Some squatter was staying in my cabin and graffitied the wall. I saw someone in an orange jacket stare at me one time—I don't even *know* if they chased me or if I panicked and went back to that day, and the rest of it just happened in my head. What exactly am I going to tell them?"

"The letters alone are enough—"

"*No*. If I do that, it gets back in the news and those horrible gossip rags. They're still sending letters to my old house. They don't know where I live. I'm *not* dredging it all up again. In fact, now that I've told you, now that I've said it out loud, it doesn't sound that bad at all," Cally said.

Laurie didn't say anything for a moment. She stared at the glow from the wood burner. Cally was afraid she'd annoyed her. She stayed silent and waited on the sofa for a storm to kick off.

Laurie looked at her then. Her eyes were kind, but Cally still flinched when she reached for her hand again.

"Sorry," Cally said.

"Don't be. What did you think I was going to do?" Laurie asked.

Cally shrugged. She *really* didn't want to get into all *that*. "What are you thinking?"

Laurie let it go and took Cally's hand. "I was thinking you've lived with this for a while now, and you obviously know best. But would you promise me one thing?"

Cally waited, her hand cold in Laurie's warm one.

"Cally, if things get worse, or if anything else happens, would you tell me? Would you let me help you?"

Cally wasn't expecting that. "I can do that," she said.

Laurie smiled. "Thank you. And if you change your mind and decide you do want to go to the police, I can go with you. Whatever you want to do, okay?"

Cally smiled back and nodded. This was different. She hadn't had this before. Jules would have walked all over whatever Cally wanted and kicked off if Cally had shown any dissent. Jules ran a tight ship.

Laurie, on the other hand, seemed happy to let Cally take the lead and accepted that Cally didn't want to do anything about it for now.

"Okay," Cally said. "Thank you."

Laurie squeezed Cally's hand, then let go. "We were going to have crème brûlée."

"What do you mean *were*?" Cally appreciated Laurie changing the subject and tried to lighten the mood. "You promised me crème brûlée. I got my hopes up."

Laurie rolled her eyes. "You are *demanding*."

Cally laughed and followed Laurie into the kitchen.

Chapter Twenty-three

Cally drove home, full of stew and crème brûlée, feeling lighter than she had in a long time. The evening had been a good one. Despite the heavy conversation when Cally told Laurie about Jules, she'd had a nice time. They didn't speak about Jules or any of the other stuff again that evening. Cally wondered if Laurie would bring it up or if she would wait for Cally to. Cally wasn't sure, but she was beginning to understand Laurie and understand that she meant the things she said.

Cally liked that. She tried not to get carried away. She wasn't ignorant of her feelings, of how she saw Laurie, that she was attracted to her. She knew she needed to be careful not to let things go somewhere she wasn't ready for. Not that Laurie had done anything this evening that told Cally she wanted more than friendship. Except…except Cally noticed her looking a few times, didn't she? In moments when Laurie thought Cally wasn't paying attention—not that Laurie had been ogling her. And not that she hadn't liked Laurie looking at her the way she did.

Cally shook her head. No, she would nip this in the bud. She was an adult—they both were—and she could admit she was attracted to Laurie and that she thought Laurie might also be attracted to her too. But that was as far as it was going right now. Besides, after what Cally'd told her tonight, she wouldn't blame Laurie if she didn't want to take Cally on. A *lot* of baggage there.

Something to the left caught Cally's eye, and she slowed down. She was driving parallel to her property, and off in the distance, near the wood, she saw the glow of a light between the trees. It bobbed along once or twice, then flicked off. Cally stopped her car and waited. Nothing. The torch—if that's what it was—didn't turn on again.

Cally started driving again and in a few minutes turned onto her long, winding drive. She kept watch on the woods out of the corner of her eye, unsure what to do. It was definitely a torchlight she'd seen—she was sure of it.

The question was, who was out by her cabins, and what were they doing? Cally wondered if it might be the same person who'd been staying in her cabin. Were they breaking into another one to flood it and deface the walls?

Whatever they were doing, there was no way she was going out there to check. She wasn't stupid. This was definitely one for the police. Whoever it was out there, they were trespassing. Cally dug her phone out of her bag and called the police.

It didn't take them long to come out, and Cally waited in her car with the doors locked. She saw the marked car come up the drive with its blue light lazily blinking on and off. Cally felt relieved.

She got out of her car and met the two officers, one male and one female.

"Hello, I'm Cally Pope. The one who called."

They greeted her politely. The female one asked Cally to go over what she'd told them on the phone.

"I was driving past, and I saw a torchlight over by my cabins. Earlier today I discovered someone living there. They've vandalised the wall and possibly it was them who flooded one of the other cabins."

The officers nodded. They told her to go and wait in the house while they walked down and looked around.

As soon as Cally got indoors, she could feel the thermostat was turned down again. The house was bloody freezing.

"Fuck's sake," Cally hissed and twisted the dial back up to twenty-five. She hit the hall light switch and saw straight away something was wrong. Muddy footprints all the way up the hall led upstairs.

Cally didn't hesitate—she went straight back out the front door and got into her car. She locked the doors and waited. She looked up at the windows on the first floor, but she knew she wouldn't see anyone. Whoever had been in her house was gone. She'd seen their torchlight in the wood.

Cally tried to keep the panic down. What the bloody hell? Her good feeling from earlier was gone now, replaced by dread and fear and anger.

Cally leaned her head back against the rest and closed her eyes.

Click clunk.

Cally's eyes flew open. Someone had unlocked her car. She punched down on the lock button again, panic bubbling up from her chest and into her throat. Her mouth was dry. *What the fuck*?

Click clunk.

Unlocked again. Cally looked frantically around. She fumbled with the lever and turned the headlights on full beam. To the left, by the side of her house, stood a figure in orange. They held their arm out.

Click clunk.

Cally couldn't help it.

She screamed.

Chapter Twenty-four

Nine months ago

Cally ran straight into the pub on the corner and barely noticed the startled stares. She heard the plunk of pool balls and the robotic blare of a fruit machine. In the corner a football match was on the TV.

Cally went straight up to the barmaid, who held a pint glass in one hand while her other hand was on a beer pump.

"*You've got to help me please call the police call them now*," Cally said on a single breath.

To her credit the barmaid put down the glass and pulled her phone out of her pocket. Behind Cally, the pub door opened again. Cally didn't need to turn to know it was Jules. Of course it was. She'd never let Cally go—Cally knew that now. She was stupid to think it might have been any other way.

"Cally," Jules said.

Cally didn't answer. In a feat of acrobatics that surprised even her, she vaulted over the bar, sending beer mats and glasses skittering to the floor.

"Call the police, please," Cally begged the barmaid.

"Already calling," the barmaid said. "There's the office behind you—go and wait in it. It locks."

"That's ridiculous," Jules said in her calm *I know what's best for you* voice. "I don't know what she's told you, but I'm her wife. It's all a misunderstanding."

Cally watched the barmaid eye Jules coolly. "Oh yeah? So why are you holding a knife?"

Cally and Jules seemed to notice it for the first time together. Jules looked from the barmaid to Cally then back again. For the first time since she'd known her, Jules looked unsure. Even in her terror, Cally felt a savage satisfaction. No talking her way out of it this time. Cally saw someone at a nearby table holding up their phone, obviously recording. They must have recognised Jules.

Jules looked at the phone then down at the knife in her hand. She dropped it. Then she turned and ran out of the pub.

Cally's legs buckled, and the barmaid grabbed her arm. "Steady there. Go in the office like I said. He's filming *you* now." The barmaid nodded at the man with the phone.

Cally managed to make her legs move. She went in the office and shut the door. She didn't lock it.

The police arrived in minutes, the press not long after that, and when the video of Jules in the pub with a knife went viral, the circus really came to town.

Cally had to leave her house—not that she would have gone back. Jules was missing. They were looking for her at the seaports and airports, but Cally knew she wouldn't be stupid enough to leave straight away. There were a million places she could go. She had money, after all, lots of it. One newspaper offered Cally six figures to do a tell-all story, but she refused. She'd rather starve, and she told them *that* too.

When Jules still hadn't been located after three days, and every place Cally could think to tell them about was searched and searched again, Cally began to wonder if she really had gone abroad. How else was she surviving without using any of her bank or credit cards? Cally had never known Jules to keep much cash around.

Then the news came. It was a Thursday afternoon, and Cally was sitting in her hotel room watching some crap daytime TV game show. There was a knock at the door. It was the police Family Liaison Officer—Cally didn't know how she'd have gotten through the last couple of days without her.

Cally saw her face and knew they'd found Jules. Except they hadn't—not exactly. They'd found her car and her jacket in a car park on Beachy Head, a notorious spot for the suicidal because there was no barrier at the cliff edge. You could walk across the grass and straight off the side into the sea, probably hitting a few rocks on the way down.

The police sent out boats and divers, but everyone knew they probably weren't going to find her. They searched for two weeks. They built a picture for Cally of what happened. Jules had been staying in a house in Eastbourne. Cally knew the friend but didn't know she was currently away in Australia filming a reality show. Jules *had* known, though. She'd also had a key to get in, which Cally learned was because they'd been having an affair.

Jules had used the woman's computer to search for the best defence barristers in London and how many people get off for attempted murder. Later searches were for routes out of the UK, how you could tell a passport was fake, and painless ways to kill yourself.

That had been Jules's final search.

The third week after they'd found Jules's car, Cally decided to move. She also decided to do her best to forget Jules ever existed.

Then the letters came.

Chapter Twenty-five

Now

For a moment, Cally couldn't move. The figure stood there, holding out the car key like some kind of trophy. They took one step forward, and Cally felt the sense come flooding back into her. She leaned on the car horn and was satisfied when the figure in orange jumped. Cally thought savagely that the fucker wasn't expecting that.

The sound of the car horn flooded the silent night and sent startled birds up out of their trees and into the sky. The figure in orange turned and ran around the side of the house.

Cally didn't let up on the horn and was relieved when she saw the officers running full pelt towards her. One of them was speaking into their radio.

Cally finally let go of the horn and got out of the car. She started talking before she reached the officers. "He went around the side of the house. He has my car key," she said.

The officers told her to get in their car. Once she was inside they locked her in. She watched them disappear around the side of the house in the same direction the figure in orange had gone.

Cally waited. It seemed like ages but the clock on the dashboard showed it was only five minutes before they came back. They had someone with them. Cally squinted into the dark. It looked like Laurie.

One of the officers unlocked the car doors and Cally jumped out. "I think you've made a mistake," she said. "That's my friend, Laurie."

Laurie was positioned between the officers with her hands cuffed in front of her. "You know her?" one of the officers asked.

"Yes. She's a friend. Laurie, I'm so sorry. I—wait. Why are you here?" Cally asked, her heart dropping. She felt sick.

"What do you mean, what am I doing here? *You* fucking messaged me. What are *you* doing, Cally?"

"That's enough," one of the officers said. "I already told you, you're under caution."

"Under caution?" Cally asked. "Why? What?"

Two more police cars came tearing up the lane, and Cally was hit by a terrible sense of déjà vu. The last time she'd seen this many police was the day Jules chased her from her house.

They'd arrested Laurie. Why? Because they found her wandering around behind the house. Why was she behind the house? If she'd come to check on Cally, wouldn't she have come up the drive in her truck? Cally felt sick. Was it Laurie? This whole time?

Cally watched as they took her to a police van that had just arrived and put her inside. She stood there numbly as they drove Laurie away.

Someone spoke to her about going to a friend's house for the night. They talked about forensic opportunities in her house and down at the cabins and a lot of other things she didn't want to think about. They asked again about a friend, anyone she could stay with? Cally shook her head, she couldn't think of anyone. She had no friends. Then she remembered Sian. But did she want to bring Sian into this? She'd met her once—could she trust her?

Cally didn't know. In the end, she decided to drive to a hotel. She could think about things in the morning. Right now, all she wanted to do was sleep.

She drove to a hotel about forty minutes away. Cally thought it was far enough away for no one to recognise her. Not that she was under any illusions the rumour mill hadn't already started. As soon as she got into the clean, bland room, her phone pinged with a text message. She hadn't looked at her phone since before she left Laurie's house, and when she checked it now she saw there were four missed calls and six texts. She'd never been so popular, Cally thought bitterly.

She checked the messages first and felt sick all over again when she saw four were from Laurie. Her first thought was how she could be contacting Cally when she'd been arrested. Then Cally saw they were all sent before she got arrested. She scrolled through them.

The first asked Cally to text her to let her know she'd got home safe. Cally snorted. Safe? When Laurie already knew that was the last thing she'd be. Sicko.

The second text was sent only a few minutes before Cally called the police. Laurie wanted Cally to call her as soon as possible, wanted to know what was going on. The final two said the same thing. Cally hit play on the voicemails and was startled to hear Laurie's voice sound pissed off. She asked what game Cally was playing. Where was she? None of it made sense. In the final voicemail, Laurie sounded scared. She said she could see the lights from the police cars and wanted to know if Cally was all right. She said she was nearly at Five Oaks.

Cally sat heavily on the bed. The springs creaked under her weight. What was going on? None of it made sense. The messages, the voicemails, was that just Laurie covering her tracks? Trying to send Cally mad? Or did she really have nothing to do with what happened tonight?

Cally's head ached and her eyes burned. It felt like she was reliving a nightmare. Jules was dead but someone else had neatly stepped into her shoes. Someone exactly like her, someone who played the same games and got the same satisfaction in scaring Cally and making her think she was losing her fucking mind.

Was she losing her mind? The messages and voicemails sounded like Laurie thought Cally had contacted her. Had she? She didn't remember sending any messages. And the figure in the orange jacket had definitely been there, outside her house. Was it Laurie, or someone else? It was impossible to tell whether the figure in orange was male or female in that baggy jacket. They didn't seem very tall, but Cally didn't know for sure—it wasn't exactly the thing she'd focussed on either time she'd seen them.

She couldn't think straight, couldn't make her heart beat settle or her leg stop jiggling. She felt like she was losing her mind. Maybe she was. Probably she was.

Whether she was or not, she needed to call the police. She needed to tell them about Laurie's messages. They'd arrested her, and it might be that she hadn't done anything. It might be that someone else was pulling the strings in this head fuck. She didn't know, *she didn't know*. And she was so tired. All she wanted to do was sleep. She didn't think she'd ever been this tired.

Before she crawled under the covers and hid from the world,

Cally called the police and told them about Laurie. She didn't know if Laurie was involved or not, but they should know about the calls and messages.

Cally didn't even take off her clothes. She pushed off her shoes at least and got under the covers. She slept with the light on, though.

Chapter Twenty-six

Cally woke up and at first couldn't think why she felt so full of dread. Then she remembered. Last night.

She groaned and rolled over in the hotel bed, pulling the covers completely over her head. She wanted to stay here and not get up. Ever. She could order room service and watch mind-numbing game shows for the rest of her life.

Cally sighed. That wasn't really practical. She kicked off the covers, got up, and went into the small, blindingly white bathroom. She ran the shower as hot as she could take it and got in. The water went some way to making her feel human again. She twisted the lid off the tiny bottle of shampoo-cum-shower gel, sniffed it, then dumped it over her head.

Along with the tiny shampoo, the hotel also provided a tiny toothbrush and tiny toothpaste—were their clientele exclusively Borrowers? Still, it was better than nothing, and even though she put on her clothes from last night—clothes she'd slept in—she felt marginally better than when she woke up.

Cally checked her phone and saw two missed calls—she'd never been so fucking popular. She knew who they were from, though. The police. Cally also noticed there was nothing from Laurie. Maybe she was still at the police station. Cally sat on the bed, braced herself, then hit redial.

The officer she spoke to was polite and friendly, and Cally thanked her for her time before hanging up. She wasn't sure whether to feel relieved or disappointed. They'd let Laurie go with no charge. That was good because it meant that Laurie had nothing to do with what happened, but bad because it also meant the figure in the orange jacket was still out there.

The officer told her they hadn't found anything forensically useful inside her house or at the cabins. They'd taken a shoe impression from the mud that had been tracked into her house, but without something to compare it with, it was useless. It had also not matched Laurie's shoes.

They found evidence of someone having been inside another of the cabins. The door was forced open, and the bathroom sink had been ripped off the wall. The officers had turned off the stopcock to stop flooding. They'd also found a can of spray paint on the floor, unused. They thought they must have disturbed whoever had been about to use it.

The one thing they did tell her, the thing that flooded her mouth with saliva and made her feel like she might be sick, was that when Laurie showed them every message on her phone, the last one she'd received was from Cally asking her to come quickly. Asking her to cut across the forest and come on foot because Cally had found a family of wild boar in the wood by the cabins and didn't want to scare them off.

Except Cally had never messaged her.

Cally didn't even know you *could* cut through the forest from Laurie's to hers. She confirmed her telephone number to the officer and it matched the one that messaged Laurie. Someone had cloned her phone. Which meant someone might have been inside her house while she was there because she took her phone everywhere.

The idea of it made her go cold. Someone in her house and her with no clue. Another idea occurred to her then, and this time she ran to the bathroom and threw back the toilet lid. She retched and gagged.

The thermostat. It had been turned down to ten each time Cally went out and came home. Maybe there was no fault at all. Maybe whoever had come into her house and cloned her phone had also turned the thermostat down. Why, though? To fuck with her.

Someone who knew Jules liked it at ten degrees. Someone who knew Jules had watched her. Someone who had an orange jacket just like Jules on the day she broke into Cally's house. Someone *just like* Jules? Or Jules?

Cally sat back on her heels and wiped her mouth. Now, instead of feeling sick she was angry. So fucking angry. Whether it was Jules or not, someone was messing with her. Trying to scare her. Was she going to sit back and be passive just like she'd been in her marriage, or was she going to fight back?

Cally decided she knew the answer to that. When she'd bought Five Oaks, she swore she'd never allow herself to be frightened in her own home again. That she would never allow someone to rule her or threaten her or control her ever again. She'd broken free of Jules once, and she'd do it again.

Cally swilled from the tiny bottle of mouthwash on the side, then went back in the bedroom and started making calls.

CHAPTER TWENTY-SEVEN

Cally pulled up outside her house and sat for a moment. It looked the same. She tried to find that feeling of safety and contentment she'd always got from looking at the place. She couldn't find it yet, but she was certain it was in there somewhere. Once she'd got everything in place—a result of all the phone calls she'd made and the huge expense she'd gone to this morning—she was certain Five Oaks would feel like hers again.

She'd spent the morning sitting on the bed in her hotel room calling around security companies. She finally found one who would come out today and—for an eyewatering amount of money—install alarms, locks, security cameras, movement sensors…the works. They also did private security, and with her battered credit card, she arranged for a team to do drive-bys each night on her property and take a walk around the cabins.

Cally told herself it was worth it. Now the police were involved, and after what happened last night, she couldn't pretend it was just another weirdo sending her hate mail from their bedroom. Whoever this was had found her in Halesbrook. That was a long way from London. And a long time to hold a grudge. Of course, the two things might not be connected. That was the hardest thing, the not knowing. Cally guessed whoever was doing this, wanted that. They wanted her to be unsure and isolated and alone.

Which brought Cally to another matter. Laurie.

Cally tried to unpick her feelings about Laurie. To all intents and purposes, she had nothing to do with this and had been used—set up.

On the other hand, Cally didn't actually *know* her. They'd hung out once, and she seemed nice, but then, so had Jules in the beginning.

Even so, Cally knew she needed to contact Laurie. The police told her they'd released Laurie with no charges and no bail—they weren't looking at her at all for this. Cally had an idea Laurie wouldn't call her first. Why would she? Cally wouldn't if she'd been in Laurie's position. No, it was up to Cally to make the first move.

If she wanted.

The thing was, she wasn't sure if she did. Laurie was complicated, especially now. She made Cally feel things, and Cally didn't think she was anywhere near ready for that. Sian was a much safer bet for friendship.

But Cally owed it to Laurie to at least speak to her. The last time they'd seen each other, Laurie was being carted away by the police.

Well, she couldn't sit here all day. She had to get out of her car at some point. Except she didn't move. She wanted to, but she couldn't get her legs to play ball. She needed to get herself together. She needed to go inside—once she'd done it the first time it would get easier. Except all she could think about was the figure in orange standing there with her car key in their hand, unlocking her car while she sat in it.

Cally closed her eyes and took a deep breath. "Fuck," she said out loud. She took her phone out.

"Hello?" Cally said when Laurie picked up after a couple of rings.

"Hi, Cally." Laurie sounded cautious and cool, and Cally couldn't blame her.

"How are you?" Cally asked and immediately felt stupid and insensitive. "Sorry, obviously you aren't okay."

"I'm good. Glad to be home," Laurie said.

"Laurie, I'm so sorry. It wasn't me who messaged you last night, and I'm just so sorry you got caught up in all this," Cally blurted out.

"I know it wasn't you. The police told me. You don't need to apologise," Laurie said.

"I do, though. If it wasn't for me, none of this would have happened. The stuff that went on in London, I've brought it here somehow. I don't know why someone wants to hurt me—"

"Cally, I said it's okay. I'm actually surprised you called me. I wasn't sure if you would after what happened."

"Look, Laurie, I admit that last night, I thought it was you. When they brought you from around the house…"

"It didn't look good, I know that."

"But I should have trusted you," Cally said.

"Why? You hardly know me," Laurie replied.

Cally didn't know what to say. She wasn't used to this. To someone who was reasonable, someone who didn't blame her when things went wrong. "I think you're being too nice to me. I got you arrested."

Laurie laughed. "Well, I don't think that's completely true. Besides, they let me go."

They did let Laurie go. So Cally should just accept that. She really *wanted* to accept that. But did she trust Laurie? No. How could she? Like Laurie said herself, Cally hardly knew her. God, she wanted to, though.

"Cally, are you still there?" Laurie asked.

"Yes. It's good they let you go."

"Really? Because you don't sound like you think it's good," Laurie said.

"I am glad. It's just…"

"Whoever it was last night is still out there. I don't think you should stay at your place alone."

Cally wanted to tell Laurie not to worry, that her house was about to become Fort Knox in the next couple of hours. Something stopped her, though. That trust thing.

"Look, Cally, I'm not saying you should stay with me or I should stay with you. After what happened, I don't think that's a good idea. But I know Sian would probably come over."

Cally pretended to consider it. "That's a thought."

"You're humouring me," Laurie said.

Cally laughed. "Maybe a little."

Laurie sighed down the phone. "Well, at least think about it. What did the police say?"

Again, something in Cally bristled at the question. Wondered at Laurie wanting to know.

"Sorry. None of my business," Laurie said.

"I mean, getting arrested probably makes it your business. They have no leads. They took the letters last night and are going to look into them. In the meantime, they're checking CCTV in the area and speaking to people. There isn't really much else they can do."

"I suppose not."

Neither of them spoke for a minute. Cally couldn't keep track of all the things she was feeling about Laurie. She desperately wanted to trust her, wanted to believe her, wanted to lean on her. Cally thought Laurie probably would let her too.

"Laurie?"

"Yeah?"

"I'm sitting in my car on the drive. I'm afraid to go in my own house." It cost Cally a lot to say this, and she wanted to take it back as soon as it was out of her mouth.

"Hang on, I'm coming now," Laurie said.

CHAPTER TWENTY-EIGHT

Laurie's familiar truck pulled up behind her, and Cally couldn't believe it was only last night they were eating dinner and enjoying each other's company at Laurie's house. Fast-forward fourteen hours, and here they were—Laurie released from custody this morning and Cally not able to shake the feeling she was still guilty somehow.

Cally got out of her car at the same time as Laurie, and they met in an awkward kind of half hug, half pat on the back.

"Thanks for coming," Cally said.

"Yeah, of course," Laurie said. "Did you want me to go in and look around first?" she asked, nodding at the house.

Cally turned to look up at it. So many windows stared blankly down at her, blank and shadowed. Anyone could be standing in any of the rooms right now, and she wouldn't know.

The last thing she wanted to do was go inside. "No, let's go in together. Safer with two of us," Cally said.

Laurie nodded. "You have your keys?"

"Yes." Cally took them out and clutched them in her hand like some kind of talisman. She wasn't sure why it helped to hold them so tight, but it did. She slipped the end of one key through her first and middle knuckles. She'd seen it on TV once.

Together, they walked up to the house. Cally unlocked it, then stepped aside as Laurie walked past her into the hall.

"Cold in here," she said and looked around.

Cally could see the muddy footprints were still on the floor and that the light switches and hall table had a fine film of dust on them. "I need to clean it. The police said it was okay to now."

"I'll help," Laurie said. "Once we've looked around."

Just like several nights ago, Cally followed Laurie from room to room and was relieved when she saw everything was as she'd left it. The figure in orange had been inside—probably many times—but last night, it didn't seem as if they'd had much of a chance to do anything. Or maybe they'd planned only to leave the footprints. Probably that was enough.

By the time they got to the kitchen, Cally was feeling better. She still didn't feel okay, not like before. Her house didn't feel like her sanctuary any more, and she damned that orange fucker for it.

Cally slammed two mugs onto the side by the kettle. "Tea?" she asked Laurie.

"I'm not sure what the right answer is," Laurie said from the table.

"What do you mean?" Cally spun around.

Laurie leaned back in her chair and held up her hands. "Don't shoot, I'm unarmed."

Cally rolled her eyes. "I'm not mad at you."

"Well, that's a relief. Yes please—to the tea," Laurie said.

"I'm mad at that bastard in the orange jacket. He—they—*whoever*—has ruined this house for me," Cally said and shoved two teabags into the mugs.

"That's a reasonable way to feel," Laurie said. "Anyone would, under the circumstances. They told me, in my interview, what happened."

"I'm so sorry you've been dragged into it," Cally said. "I don't understand why they're doing it. I mean, if it's the same person sending the letters—"

"I think it's safe to assume it is," Laurie said.

Cally nodded. She poured hot water in the mugs and gave the teabags a stir. "Me too. I know they think I'm responsible for Jules's death, but that doesn't explain all this. Why not just, I don't know, stab me or whatever?"

Laurie accepted the mug from Cally and took a sip. She didn't speak for a moment, but her brow was furrowed in a way Cally was coming to realise meant she was thinking. "We're assuming this person is a stalker, right?" Laurie asked.

Cally nodded. "Of a sort, I suppose."

"No, I think they're pretty much a bona fide stalker. They're obsessed with you. They've followed you all the way up here. They wait around outside your house. They've been *inside* your house. They cloned your phone and vandalised your cabins."

"Yes," Cally said and sat down at the table. She took a sip of tea from her own mug.

"Don't they work up to the stabbing part?"

"It's been nine months already since Jules died."

"Can't these things go on for years?" Laurie asked.

Cally felt sick all over again. She couldn't stand years of this. "I suppose that's true."

"What have the police said?" Laurie asked.

"They've advised me to move out for a bit. Change the locks, get cameras, all that stuff. I can't—no, I *won't* move. The rest is being done today," Cally said.

"Do you think you might know the person doing it?" Laurie asked.

"At the beginning, I wondered if it was someone I knew. Or someone Jules knew. They had my address. But it was only the letters then, just blaming me, saying it was my fault Jules died, and I might as well have pushed her off the cliff myself. It's only since I moved here that things got…scary."

Laurie nodded. "So, there's a chance it isn't the same person? That *this* might be totally unrelated to *that*."

"It's possible. *Anything's* possible. That's what makes it so awful. I don't know who it is or why they're doing it."

"Is there anyone from London you didn't get on with? Any run-ins, something like that?" Laurie asked.

Cally shook her head. "No. I didn't have any friends left by the time Jules died. I knew some of hers, but I wouldn't have called them friends. They were people to be seen with and photographed with. They came and went. Jules never seemed to particularly *like* any of them, and I didn't get the sense they were hugely fond of her."

"What about…I mean, I know it came out after that the house she was hiding in—"

"She was having affairs, yes," Cally said. Strangely, she didn't feel one way or the other about it now. At first, when she'd been told, when she'd found letters and messages and bank statements and photographs in Jules's office, it had hurt. Floored her, really. All those years Jules accused Cally of being unfaithful, when all the time she had been putting it about like her vagina was having a closing-down sale. "There were a lot of women. I couldn't even tell you how many."

"Was there anyone…I don't know, *special*?" Laurie looked uncomfortable when she said it, and Cally smiled and reached across the table to take her hand.

"You don't need to worry about my feelings. Any love or care I had for Jules died a long time before she did. As to whether there was someone special, I'd have to say no. She kept a diary, like a journal. I think she thought she was Anne Lister or something." Cally rolled her eyes, remembering the heavy, clunking, flowery prose. Laurie had Jules's memoirs on her bookcase, and she'd be surprised to see how much work the ghostwriter actually did. Jules was no Brontë sister.

"It mentioned other women?" Laurie asked.

"That's one way of putting it. But there was no one in there that sounded like she meant anything—I could be wrong, but I knew Jules. She didn't love anyone more than she loved herself. I think she saw everyone in her life as there purely to serve her needs. I don't think it occurred to her that anyone else had actual feelings."

"She was a narcissist," Laurie said.

Cally nodded. "I think there are a lot of people described that way, when actually they're just selfish. For Jules, though, it sums her up perfectly."

"I'm sorry. That must have been impossible to live with."

Cally smiled. "It was. That's why I left her."

"And now, you're still being drawn into something that revolves around her," Laurie said.

Cally smiled, but she had to try for it. She was so tired. "I suppose I am. The fact is, it could be anyone doing this stuff."

Laurie picked at a wood knot in the table. "This will sound crazy, but do you think—"

"That Jules faked her own death?" Cally asked. It was a relief that someone else had the same thought. "I think that all the time. Usually at night when I'm trying to sleep."

"Is it possible?"

"I really don't know. They didn't find her body, but they seemed to be convinced she jumped off Beachy Head. Plus, wouldn't someone have seen her by now? She was all over the TV and in every magazine. She's recognisable. Also, what would she be doing for money?" As soon as Cally said it, she thought about her cabin, where someone had obviously been staying.

"Just an idea," Laurie said.

"Anything's possible. I just don't see it as something Jules would do. She was so full of herself that I don't think she'd have been able to stay quiet for nine whole months."

Laurie was about to say something when the sound of a vehicle outside made them both jump. Cally noticed Laurie followed her into the hall, staying close behind, and she appreciated it.

When Cally looked through the front room window, she saw it was the security people and was relieved.

"That's good," Laurie said from behind her. "Shall I go?"

"Do you mind staying?" Cally asked. There was something about Laurie that made her feel better being in this house, which made no sense when she still didn't trust her.

"Of course not."

"Thank you," Cally said.

She opened the front door to let the workmen in.

Chapter Twenty-nine

When the banging and drilling started, Cally decided it was time to get out of the house. She wanted to go back down to the cabins and leave more food out for the stray dog. She thought if Laurie came with her, there would be safety in numbers at least if the orange fucker was still hanging about.

"What dog? Do you have a dog?" Laurie asked, trying to be heard above the noise.

Cally shut the kitchen door. "No, she's a stray. She's living in one of the cabins. If you won't tell me where the nearest pet shop is, I'll just google it."

Laurie rolled her eyes. "Of course I'll tell you. I'm not against dogs. Why don't you just call the council, though? They'll come and take her away."

Cally hesitated to answer. Before it all kicked off yesterday, she was struggling with the same thought. The sensible thing would be to call the dog warden, not try to befriend the dog. But something about the dog made Cally want to help her. She probably saw her own helplessness in the dog.

"I'm not getting into a whole conversation with you about it. Are you going to help me or not?" Cally asked.

Laurie laughed. "That told me. Yeah, fine. I'll drive you to the pet shop and then we can go and feed your mangy dog."

Getting to the pet shop was easy. It was trying to pick food where Cally got stuck. Laurie was no help either. Every time Cally asked her if she thought the dog had a sensitive stomach, or would prefer gravy, Laurie shrugged.

"With all due respect, Cally, it's a stray. I'm pretty sure she'll be happy with whatever you feed her."

"But I want to get something she'll like. Something that tastes good."

Laurie nodded. "And then what? You feed her for a bit, she becomes friendly, what happens next?"

"I'm not sure," Cally lied. In her mind, she had visions of long walks around the glamping site with the dog at her heels. Cuddling up on the sofa in the winter. She was too embarrassed to tell Laurie, though, because it sounded stupid.

"Oh, you liar. You've got all sorts of little Lassie dreams in your head, haven't you?" Laurie said.

"No, I have not," Cally lied again.

Laurie snorted. "Yes, you do. You've got visions of frolicking in the meadows and skipping through the forest with your faithful mutt at your side."

Cally couldn't help it, she laughed. "Piss off. So, what if I do?"

Laurie grinned. "Then I say, good for you. That mutt could probably do with a bit of human kindness. Here, look, this food is one hundred percent meat and prepared by virgins. I reckon it'll do your furry little squatter."

Cally put it in the trolley. While she was here, she might as well buy her a proper bed and decent dishes to eat out of.

By the time they got back to Five Oaks after a brief stop so Cally could buy a new phone, it was after three, and the security people were still hammering and drilling away. Cally and Laurie headed down to the cabins with the dog food, dishes, and a large warm bed, which had cost a fortune. With that and what she was spending on the new security, it had turned out to be a pretty expensive day.

The sight of the wood and the cabins didn't fill Cally with the same sort of joy they had only a day ago. Instead, a feeling of dread settled in the pit of her stomach, and the shadows between the trees made her uneasy.

"You okay?" Laurie asked.

"Of course. No, that's a lie. It feels tainted here," Cally said.

"I bet. Listen, don't let whoever this is mess things up for you. This is the most beautiful part of your property," Laurie said.

Cally nodded. "I know. I'm trying."

Cally tried not to look at the broken and splintered doors of the cabins they walked past. Instead she focused on the way the weak winter sun valiantly tried to poke through the dense evergreens. It really was beautiful here.

"I didn't know you could walk from my property to yours through the forest," Cally said.

Laurie nodded. "From your attic, you can see the roof of my house. It's longer to drive it. But more convenient. Easy to get lost if you don't know the way."

Cally stopped.

"What?" Laurie asked.

Cally looked at her. Tried to get a read on her. "How do you know that?"

"Know what?" Laurie asked.

"How do you know you can see the roof of your house from my attic?" Cally asked. She could feel her chest tighten. She looked around and realised how totally isolated they were. You couldn't even see her house from here.

"Cally." Laurie took a step towards her.

"No, don't. Stay away from me," Cally said.

"Are you fucking serious?" Laurie dropped the cans of dog food on the ground. "Do you *actually* think I'm the one stalking you?"

"I don't know," Cally said. And honestly, she didn't. She didn't want to believe it was Laurie, but when had Laurie been in Cally's attic? And she even said it was quicker to walk through the forest than drive between their houses. Wasn't it possible that she'd left at the same time as Cally last night? Wasn't it possible she'd been in the woods just as Cally drove by and saw her torchlight?

"Do you know what? I don't need this, Cally. I really don't. You obviously know something the police don't because they let me go this morning. And I didn't blame you for last night. I really didn't. But this? *This* is too much. Good luck with your dog."

Laurie walked past Cally without another look and headed back towards the house. Cally watched her go. She watched her until she was out of sight and out of the wood and until she was sure Laurie *had* gone back to the house.

Cally picked up the dog food Laurie dropped and carried on towards the cabin. She tried not to think about what she'd just done.

CHAPTER THIRTY

Cally was pleased to see the dog had used the blankets and towels she'd laid out for her. They were in a muddy tangle, so she straightened them out. She put down food and water and left. She wanted to go back into the cabin's bedroom and look at those eyes again, but she stopped herself. No good could come of it.

Cally stepped out of the cabin and into the dappled sunshine. Today was the kind of day to sit in the garden with a blanket and read a book, but she didn't have time for that. What she had were a million emails to read and reply to. She had washing to do in the house, and she needed to clean up. Cally hoped all those things would take her mind off what happened just now with Laurie.

She started the walk back up to the house. Behind her, twigs snapped. Cally turned quickly, expecting a blur of orange to come barrelling at her. Instead, she saw the dog. She stood some way off to the left of the cabin, and she watched Cally.

Instinctively, Cally crouched down. "Hey, girl," she said softly, trying to make her voice gentle. The dog lifted its nose and sniffed the air, likely trying to get Cally's scent.

"I left you some food," Cally said, and the dog tilted her head to one side. "Here, girl. Will you come and say hi?" Cally asked.

To her surprise, the dog stepped towards her, eyes locked on Cally. "I won't hurt you," she felt compelled to say even though the dog wouldn't understand. It really was a lovely dog. Cally didn't know much about breeds, but this one looked like a dog she'd seen in a film once. What was it called? A German shepherd maybe? She was big with bedraggled black and brown hair. Cally thought she was probably much too skinny under all the fur.

The dog stepped forward again, then lay down. Cally wasn't sure what to do. Should she go to her? Before she could decide, the dog's ears pricked, and she lifted her head and growled low in her throat. She stood up and looked at something behind Cally.

Cally stood too and quickly turned. Someone was coming. The dog walked to within a few feet of Cally, but her attention was on whoever was coming through the wood. She growled again. Cally was afraid. She shouldn't have come down here—that was a mistake. She looked around for something to defend herself with and came up short. Cally could feel her blood beating in her ears. The dog barked, then snarled at whatever was in the wood. It made Cally jump.

"Cally?" A disembodied voice. Cally recognised it. Just as she placed it, Sian walked into view.

"There you are," Sian said and sketched a small wave.

The dog took a couple of steps in front of Cally and growled low and savage. Instinctively, Cally put a gentle hand on the dog's back.

"Sian, thank God," she said as she felt the crushing weight of fear lift.

"I didn't know you had a dog," Sian said and looked nervously at the dog.

The dog, seeming to realise it was close to both these strange humans, turned and ran back into the wood without another glance.

"I don't, exactly. She's a stray," Cally said.

"Well, she seemed pretty protective of you," Sian said.

"I've been feeding her. She's living in one of the cabins."

Sian nodded and looked off for a moment in the direction the dog had run. Her brow was furrowed. "Well, I hope you don't mind me coming down here. I saw Laurie up at the house, and she told me where you were."

Cally nodded, trying to ignore the crawling feeling of regret Laurie's name had conjured up.

"I've offended you. I shouldn't have come down without asking first," Sian said. "I'm sorry, I—"

"No, no. You haven't offended me. It's sweet of you to come by. I should have expected this would be common knowledge by now," Cally said. "Want to come up to the house for a cup of tea?"

Sian nodded and looked relieved. "Yes, thanks. I'm really not trying to get gossip. I was worried about you."

Cally smiled and linked arms with Sian. "Thank you. I am okay, though. How was Laurie when you saw her just now?"

"She seemed all right. She said you were down in the wood by the cabins," Sian said.

"She didn't seem…pissed off?"

Sian nudged Cally and grinned. "Why? Did you two have a lovers' tiff?"

Cally rolled her eyes. "No, of course not. We aren't lovers."

"Yet," Sian said.

Cally didn't tell her that after what just happened, it was unlikely they'd ever be that. She changed the subject instead. "Who's running the bakery while you're down here with me?"

"I have staff, you know," Sian said feigning indignation.

Cally played along. "Oh, do you? Well, excuse me."

"I'm a successful business owner. This village can't get enough sticky buns."

Cally laughed. "What would they do without you?"

"Before I got here, they bought their doughnuts from supermarkets." Sian pretended to shiver.

"Outrageous. And in six short months you've built a sticky bun empire."

Sian tapped her head. "Because I'm a great businesswoman."

They approached the house, where a workman was busy fixing a camera above the front door.

"Blimey, it's like Fort Knox," Sian said.

"That's the plan," Cally said.

They went into the kitchen, and Cally put the kettle on for tea. "Sian, what exactly is going around the village?"

"Probably nothing accurate," Sian said. "A few people saw a load of police cars up here last night. Theories range from the mundane—you got burgled—to the outrageous…you got kidnapped."

Cally couldn't help it, she burst out laughing. "Kidnapped?"

Sian nodded. "Yep. On account of how you have all this money from your late wife."

"That's ridiculous. What's the most popular theory?" Cally asked.

Sian sighed. "I feel awkward telling you."

Cally handed Sian a mug of tea and sat down. "I can take it."

"Well, it was all in the news a while ago, wasn't it? About Jules Kay."

Cally nodded and braced herself.

"A few people said you've got a stalker, and that last night, they broke into your house. Apparently Laurie got arrested—except that can't be true because I just saw her. Someone said your cabins have been vandalised too."

Cally sat back and thought for a moment. The rumour mill had it pretty accurate, which she supposed was to be expected in such a small village. Even so, it felt horrible and invasive and embarrassing. She had to live with these people and try to get them to take her seriously, treat her with respect. How was she going to do that with all her dirty laundry aired for public consumption?

"Cally? I'm sorry, I didn't mean to upset you," Sian said.

"You didn't, it's fine. I'm just embarrassed, is all. I can confirm the rumours are accurate," Cally said.

"Oh right. I see. I can't imagine what it's like. What's happened is bad enough, but everyone discussing it like that…I don't know. I'd *hate* it," Sian said. "Shit, sorry. I'm being a dick."

Cally smiled. "No, you aren't. I appreciate you coming up here to tell me. At least I know everyone's talking about me."

Sian took Cally's hand and squeezed. "They'll be talking about someone else pretty soon. And you're safe—that's all that matters."

Cally nodded. "I'll feel much safer once this is all done."

"The cameras?" Sian asked.

"Cameras, alarms, locks. If anyone comes within twenty feet of the house, I'll know about it," Cally said.

"Did they get inside the house, then?" Sian asked.

Cally nodded. She didn't see the point of keeping anything to herself if everyone already knew anyway. "Trashed a couple of my cabins and poked around in here."

"God, that's terrible. Do you know who it is?"

"No."

"But they arrested Laurie? So they thought it was her?"

Cally felt a strange surge of protectiveness for Laurie. "It wasn't Laurie." Except it *could* be Laurie. Hadn't they fallen out about it earlier? Hadn't Cally basically *accused* Laurie of being responsible? Jesus, she was so confused.

"I guess it wasn't her. Not if the police let her go. And she was up here this morning," Sian said, and Cally suddenly felt like this was more than friendly concern from Sian. It sounded like she was digging.

"If it's okay, I don't think I want to talk about it any more," Cally said.

"Of course, of course. Sorry, I'm being nosy. It's none of my business," Sian said.

Now Cally felt bad. Why was she always so suspicious of everyone? She couldn't keep blaming Jules for her trust issues. If she carried on this way, she was going to lose everyone and end up alone.

"Sorry, I didn't mean that. You aren't being nosy. I'm just tired and pissed off and sick of the whole thing," Cally said.

Sian squeezed her hand again. "You know what you need?"

"What?" Cally asked.

"A night out. We should drive into Gloucester and get shit-faced," Sian said.

Cally laughed. It sounded so appealing, but she had too much to do. "I can't. I really want to, but I've got emails to send and calls to make." Her head swam with all the things she still needed to do today. "Rain check?"

Sian nodded. "Okay. But I also have a plan B up my sleeve."

"What's that?"

"I'll come over tonight when you've finished all your businessy stuff. We'll open some wine and watch some crap reality TV."

That sounded good. It would mean she wouldn't have to be alone here tonight, and maybe Sian would take her mind off everything going on. "I like that idea. Why don't you head over around seven?"

"Seven it is." Sian stood up. "I should get back to work. Those sticky buns won't sell themselves."

"I thought that's exactly what your sticky buns did," Cally said, and Sian laughed.

"Sian," Cally said.

"Yeah?"

"Thank you. For coming over today. And offering to come later too," Cally said.

"Of course," Sian replied and kissed Cally's cheek. "It's what friends do."

Cally waited until Sian drove away, then went back inside to start on her mountain of emails and phone calls.

CHAPTER THIRTY-ONE

For a day that started abysmally, it wasn't ending too badly. Cally still didn't know what to do about Laurie, but she felt like she'd earned the right to park that conundrum for another day. The good news was she was up to date on all her correspondence and phone calls. Work would start on the glamping site next week. There was still the matter of the possible challenge by Laurie and her gang, but they had no issue with the existing site and so that could begin.

The security people had turned her house into a fortress. Cally thought it would still be a while before it felt the way it did before, but she was on the way. Cameras fed directly to her phone and were triggered to start recording any time there was movement in a twenty foot circumference of the house. The locks on the windows and doors had cost a small fortune, but there was no way anyone was getting inside.

One of the security people told her the locks she'd had before were useless, and she might as well have not bothered. He showed her how easy it was to pop the catch off the front door with a good shouldering. It was frightening, really.

Now she had deadbolts and chains and tamper-proof locks. There was even a metal bar that ran down the front door frame. Cally felt safer.

Her phone buzzed with a text from Sian to say she was on her way. Cally turned on the oven to preheat and took a pizza out of the fridge. That was the other thing she'd learned about living out here. Impossible to get takeaway. She'd taken to stocking the freezer with frozen pizzas.

Cally doubted Laurie did that. Laurie probably had a pizza oven and regularly whipped up restaurant style pizzas for her guests. Cally put two bottles of white wine in the fridge and chucked some crisps in a bowl. That was about the extent of her hosting capabilities.

Her phone buzzed again, and Cally saw it was the security app. It had recorded something. Her finger shook slightly as she pressed the icon, even though she kept telling herself it was only Sian. The still image showed the back of the house. When she hit play, she saw something move between the trees. It was there one second and gone the next. Cally thought about all the things it could be. The security people said it was unlikely but possible that the sensors would pick up large animals if they got close. Maybe it was the dog?

Cally played the video again. It was impossible to really see *what* it was. She guessed this was the downside to having cameras. The paranoia must be difficult to shut down.

As soon as she put the phone down, it buzzed again. She almost didn't want to look at it. But of course, she did. This time it clearly showed someone standing at the edge of the trees at the back of her property. The footage was black and white, but she recognised the jacket, much lighter than the rest of the figure's clothes. As quickly as they appeared, the figure in orange disappeared back into the trees again.

Cally immediately dialled the police. As soon as she hung up, her phone buzzed again with another video. Her legs turned to jelly, and she sat heavily into a kitchen chair. She almost screamed when the doorbell chimed.

Cally brought up the app and almost cried with relief when she saw it was Sian. She quickly ran to the door to let her in.

"Whoa, excited to see you too," Sian said when Cally flung open the door and pulled her inside before slamming it shut again.

"Cally, what happened?" Sian asked, the grin falling off her face. "I thought you were joking."

"He was here again," Cally said.

"Who was?" Sian asked.

"The stalker or whatever you'd call him. He was stood back there, behind the house." Cally walked into the kitchen with Sian following behind. She pulled her phone out and sat down at the table. "I called the police."

"Shit, I'm so sorry. Well, I'm here now. We'll wait together."

"I feel sick," Cally said. Saliva filled her mouth, and her stomach roiled and rolled. Cally ran upstairs to the bathroom, hoping she'd make it in time.

She did, barely. Cally heaved and gagged. When she thought she'd got everything up, she sat back on her heels and wiped her mouth with the back of her hand.

"You okay?" Sian asked from behind her. Cally hadn't even known she was there. "Stupid question. Of course you aren't."

Cally turned around. "I feel strangely better now. I thought I'd be doing that much later on tonight."

Sian laughed. "If anyone deserves a drink tonight, it's you. We can get smashed."

"You don't have to stay. In fact, it might be better if you don't," Cally said.

"It's probably better if neither of us do. You can stay with me tonight," Sian said.

"No, I can't do that. I'll go to a hotel," Cally said.

"Absolutely not. I've got room at mine if you don't mind the sofa. Nick's away, so it'll just be us. We can do what we'd planned, just at my place instead."

Cally thought about it. It was a tempting offer. But being chased out of her home didn't sit well. It wasn't like the figure in orange could actually get *in*. Not now that the locks were installed. The doorbell rang and interrupted her train of thought.

"That'll be the police," Cally said and stood up.

Chapter Thirty-two

While police officers walked around her property looking for the figure in the orange jacket, Cally sat in the living room with a detective. She went over everything from the beginning. She was tired of thinking about it, of talking about it. She just wanted to get on with her life. The detective wrote things down in an A4 notebook as Cally spoke.

"And before you moved here, it was just the letters?"

"Yes," Cally said. "It's the last couple of days I've been seeing this person."

"And you have the footage of them on your phone from tonight?"

Cally nodded. She reached in her pocket for her phone to find it missing.

"It's okay," Sian said. "I think you left it in the kitchen. I'll get it."

The detective gave Cally a sympathetic look. "Rough night for you. Again."

Cally nodded. "Have you had any luck with the letters? I know I only handed them in last night."

"We're looking into a few things," the detective said. "We'll do our best to identify them."

Sian came back in with Cally's phone. Cally pressed the security app and scrolled through the videos. There were a bunch of new ones that had recorded all the police showing up and looking around.

Cally found the first one. "Here. You can't really see anyone, but there's something there."

The detective watched the video, noted the time, and nodded. "And the other one? The one that shows them standing by the trees?"

Cally knew as soon as she looked it wasn't there any more. She felt sick. It had come straight after the first one. She scrolled again, then checked the deleted folder. Gone.

"It was definitely here," Cally said. "I saw it."

The detective nodded. "That's okay. Maybe you deleted it by mistake. We can ask the company to send us a copy of it."

Cally scrolled again. And again. What the fuck was going on? It was here. It *had been* here. She *knew* it had. "Someone's wiped it off. Someone went in my phone and wiped it off." Cally saw the look Sian gave the detective.

"It really is okay, Ms. Pope. We can see if the company can send it to us."

"No. They can't. It goes to a cloud thingy. Once you delete it, you can't get it back," Cally said.

"It doesn't matter anyway. You've called us about it, and we'll put it on the report," the detective said.

Cally nodded. She was drained. How had it been deleted? She'd been out today to pick up a new phone, and no one had touched it but her. It couldn't have been cloned. That left Sian.

Sian, who was now with the detective showing her out.

Cally had no idea when she'd come up to the bathroom. Cally had left her phone on the dining table unlocked.

Cally made herself stop. She couldn't go around blaming everyone who tried to be her friend. She'd already alienated Laurie. Now she was going to do the same to Sian? She didn't know what to do. Maybe the video hadn't been there in the first place, and she was losing her mind.

Was she losing her mind?

"Cally?" Sian stood in the doorway to the living room. "Shall I get you a glass of wine?"

Cally shook her head. "No. The way I'm feeling, that's probably not a good idea."

"The detective said the officers would knock again when they'd finished looking. So far, they haven't found anyone. They're just checking the cabins again. But I guess the cameras would pick up anyone down there."

"Yes, they would. Wait, how do you know I have cameras down there?" Cally asked and was very much aware this conversation was following the same pattern as the one she'd had with Laurie. The one where she'd basically accused Laurie of stalking her.

Sian's eyes narrowed. "What are you saying?"

Cally sighed and closed her eyes. She put her head in her hands. "Nothing. Sorry. I don't know what's wrong with me."

"It's okay. I get it. You must be feeling shit-scared," Sian said. "After last night, I reckon you probably have some PTSD or something."

"Is this your way of telling me I imagined the whole thing tonight?" Cally asked.

"No. No, not at all. I just meant it takes its toll. My last boyfriend had something similar happen to him. It messed him up," Sian said.

"He had a stalker?" Cally asked.

"Not quite, but someone doing things to hurt him. It was horrible," Sian said.

"I'm sorry."

Sian shrugged. "Water under the bridge now. I really do think you should come and stay with me, though. Even if it's just for tonight."

"I'll think about it," Cally said. The truth was, she was exhausted. All she wanted to do was climb into bed and forget the whole thing. Her tired brain was waving a white flag, and she didn't have the energy to think about it any more. Maybe the video had never existed. Maybe she'd superimposed the image of the figure in orange from last night into tonight. Maybe she was losing her mind and making the whole thing up.

She didn't know. Except she *did*. She *did* know that video existed. She'd *seen* it. Which meant someone wiped it off her phone.

Sian was the only other person in the house.

Maybe she was being paranoid, and she admitted she was accusing the only two people she'd gotten to know in the village, but she wasn't mad. *Someone* was doing this to her. Until the police found out who, Cally decided she was going to keep to herself. Right now, friends were a luxury she couldn't afford.

"You know what, Sian? Do you mind if we take a rain check on tonight? I think once the police leave, I'm going to lock up and get an early night," Cally said, trying to sound brighter than she felt.

Sian looked taken aback. "Are you sure it's a good idea? Being in this house on your own?"

Cally nodded. "I'm safe here just as much as anywhere else. You said it yourself, it's like Fort Knox."

Sian nodded. "You don't trust me. You think I wiped that video off your phone."

"No. It's not that, I promise. I just want to go to bed. I'm not good company."

"I'm not stupid, Cally. But if that's what you want, I'll go." Sian stood up and walked out of the room. Cally got up to follow her.

"Sian, please. I really didn't mean to offend you."

Sian spun round, startling Cally. "You know, Cally, you need to be careful about accusing people of things. Or you won't have any friends left."

Sian opened the door, stepped out, and slammed it shut behind her. Cally heard her car start and the wheels kick up loose gravel as she drove off.

CHAPTER THIRTY-THREE

Nine months ago

Jules was pissed off. Really pissed off. How dare she? Who did she think she was, making demands like that? Like Jules was some little servant to be ordered around?

She came, though. Of course she came. It had been made all but impossible for her to do anything else *but* come. Jules knew the whole thing was a mistake, knew *she* had been a mistake. People warned her from the beginning, but here she was, waiting on a cold and windy bench in the dark. On a frigging cliff. Jules always cleaned up her messes, though, and she'd seen an opportunity and taken it. Story of her life. It was how she'd become as successful as she had.

The wind whipped around her, making her shiver, and for a moment, she felt…strange. It had been happening more and more since the *incident*. These bouts of sudden fear would hit her and make it difficult to breathe. And it wasn't that Jules wasn't familiar with the feeling of fear—she'd been scared pretty much consistently for as long as she could remember. It was that *this* fear she could almost reach out and touch.

It was right there in front of her. It was in her ruined career, her destroyed public image, in *everything* that made her Jules Kay. And there was only one person to blame.

Cally.

When Jules thought of her wife, a white hot rage paralysed her. It fired every synapse, every nerve ending, every *fibre* of her being. She hated Cally with the same passion she'd once loved her. Cally had taken everything Jules ever gave her and thrown it back in her face. Stamped the fucking life out of it.

The only thing that kept Jules going was the idea that one day she'd pay her back. She'd pay Cally back for all the pain and the hurt and the fear she'd caused Jules to suffer. When all Jules had ever done was love her. Cally had twisted that love and turned Jules into a monster. The things they were saying about her in the papers. Of course, *some* of the more decent journalists were calling bullshit on Cally's outrageous lies about her. Jules's fans were on her side too. It was the only thing that kept her going. The *only* thing that made her think she might be able to come out of this the other side.

Jules breathed in the night air. It was cold and clean—the opposite of her anger—and it calmed her. One day, Cally would pay for what she'd done. Jules would make sure of it. It might take some time, but didn't they say revenge was best served cold? All Jules had to do was get through the next half an hour or so. A little bit of pain for a lot of gain. And it wouldn't be so bad really. Jules wasn't too proud to admit she'd made a mistake with this one. But she was about to rectify that. Jules had always been one for cleaning up her own messes, and this was no different.

Jules looked over the grass towards the road and tried to pick out the headlights of her car. She'd better come. After all this, she'd better bloody come.

CHAPTER THIRTY-FOUR

Now

Cally watched the digger trundle across her lawn and down towards the field. It had been this way for the last couple of days, and she was enjoying it. Finally, things were moving forward. Things were happening with Five Oaks, even if everything else had turned to shit.

Since the evening Sian stomped out, Cally hadn't heard from her. She'd sent a couple of apologetic texts, but it didn't seem as though Sian was interested.

Cally hadn't heard from Laurie either. It seemed like her fledgling friendships were over before they'd really begun. Cally hadn't realised how much she was starting to enjoy having friends again. She hadn't messaged Laurie either. Mainly, she was embarrassed and didn't know what to say. But there was a small part of her that still wondered if Laurie or Sian was responsible for the stalking.

Cally thought it was better to keep to herself. At least until the police caught whoever was doing it. This way, she was lonely but safe.

So, the constant busyness at Five Oaks was a welcome distraction from the fact that she was alone again.

The figure in orange was leaving her alone too, and Cally hoped the combination of the new security and the police involvement might have scared them off. Whatever the reason, she was feeling better about being in the house again.

Cally was still feeding the dog, and she was getting friendlier every day. She hoped it wouldn't be long before she could coax her up to the house because work was due to start on the cabins in a couple of weeks, and the dog probably wouldn't want to hang around once that started.

Cally had decided to venture into the village today. She'd been avoiding that too after what Sian told her about all the gossiping. But she couldn't stay cooped up here forever. At some point she'd need to face people, and she'd woken up this morning and decided today was the day.

Cally was getting her boots on when she heard the familiar sound of post coming through the letterbox, thumping onto the doormat. She pushed the mild anxiety down. Since the letters started coming, the post always brought a small spike of fear.

The fear escalated when Cally spotted a letter on the floor with familiar handwriting. She supposed she'd better read it. She no longer had the luxury of bundling them up, unread, and posting them to her solicitor to deal with.

Cally was careful to handle this one by its edges, and she opened it with a letter opener so she didn't damage the seal. Inside the envelope was a plain sheet of white paper. Typed neatly in the middle was one number: *14*.

Cally didn't know what it meant, but her skin prickled just the same. The bold, black typeface seemed more sinister than all the other vile letters combined. Fourteen? Fourteen what? Days, weeks, *hours*? She didn't know what it meant, but she knew it wasn't good.

She put the paper carefully back into the envelope and got a plastic food bag from the kitchen. Cally decided she'd drop it in at the police station when she went into town.

Cally set the house alarm, turned all the locks with her uncopiable key, and went into the village.

She decided to avoid the bakery for today. Sian's unanswered messages told Cally everything she needed to know about Sian's desire to see her. Cally was already the talk of the village, and she didn't need a big ding-dong in the bakery to add to her notoriety.

Cally opted for the local grocery shop instead. It was one of those local, miniaturised versions of a supermarket that sold everything at double the price of their big brothers. But it was anonymous enough that Cally didn't think she'd be engaged in conversation.

She was wrong.

As soon as she walked in, a woman around sixty she recognised from the planning meeting came straight up to her. Cally desperately searched her memory banks for the woman's name.

"Cally, it's so nice to see you again, we've missed you in the pub," the woman said and threw Cally completely. Not that she thought anyone would just launch into questions. But this woman's overture seemed…genuine. Like she actually *was* pleased to see Cally.

"Oh well, you know…" Cally said, at a bit of a loss.

The woman nodded as though she totally understood. "You're a busy working woman. I've seen all the lorries and diggers going up to your place. The work's started, then?"

"Yes. On the tent pitches at the moment," Cally said.

The woman took Cally's hand and squeezed it warmly. "Well, as busy as you are, you need to make time to have some fun too. You're only a young woman."

Cally smiled. "I will, I promise."

"The band's playing again tomorrow night at The Colliers Arms. You should come down."

Cally thought about it. Maybe it wouldn't be such a bad idea. It was big enough that if Sian or Laurie showed up, they could easily avoid her if they wanted to. And the truth was, she was lonely. She wanted a life here and friends too. "You know what, I think I will."

The woman grinned. "Oh, good. Well, I'd better let you get on."

Cally smiled and nodded. "Good to see you again."

The woman gave Cally's hand one last squeeze and left.

Cally picked up a basket, feeling much lighter than when she came in. Maybe it wouldn't be so bad. Either the gossip had died down, or people were polite enough not to bring it up with her. She supposed tomorrow night would be the test. Lots more people and alcohol. Cally hoped that horrible woman from last time wasn't there, or at least didn't approach her.

Cally picked up a few bits and paid at the self-checkout. She stepped outside and almost walked straight into Laurie.

"Whoa." Laurie stepped back and put her arms on Cally's shoulders to steady her.

"Sorry. I was in another world," Cally said.

"No worries." Laurie wouldn't look at her.

God, this was awkward. "How have you been?" Cally asked.

Laurie nodded and looked somewhere past Cally's head. "Yeah, fine. You know. Working and stuff. You?"

"Same, really. We started work on the tent pitch field," Cally said.

Laurie nodded again. "I know. I mean, I saw the lorries and stuff going up the road. I wasn't keeping tabs or anything."

Now it was Cally's turn to look somewhere other than at Laurie. She felt ashamed. The accusation Cally made in the wood was very much between them. "Laurie, I am sorry about what happened."

"Look, Cally, I don't really want to talk about it," Laurie said.

"I understand. There's probably enough gossip as it is," Cally replied.

Laurie looked at her for the first time, and Cally saw confusion in her eyes. "I don't know about any of that. I just…I need to go. Take care, okay?"

And Laurie—who had clearly been about to walk into the shop—turned and walked in the other direction.

Cally sighed. Her feelings confused her. Part of her felt awful about accusing Laurie and the arrest and everything. But there was a small part of her that was still suspicious. A tiny part of her brain that kept telling her to be careful because Laurie might not be all that she seemed.

The sane, rational part of her realised there was just no reason for Laurie to stalk her. Cally had been getting the letters since before she'd ever met Laurie. And wouldn't it just be the strangest coincidence that she moved to the same village her stalker had lived in her whole life?

Of course, the letter writer and the stalker might not be the same person. Unlikely but still possible. Christ, she was so confused.

Cally watched Laurie walk up the road and into the bakery. Part of her wanted to follow Laurie—the insane part—and part of her wanted to get in her car and fuck off back to Five Oaks.

In the end, she got back in her car and went home.

CHAPTER THIRTY-FIVE

By the time Cally ran her other errands, it was late afternoon and the sun was beginning to dip behind the trees. She hadn't been able to stop thinking about Laurie or how they'd left things in the village earlier.

Without really thinking what she was doing, Cally found herself driving past Five Oaks and towards Laurie's house. The rational part of her brain told her to stop and turn around. She couldn't. She had a connection with Laurie. Attraction aside, Cally really *liked* her and she hated the way they'd left things. She hated that she'd made Laurie feel like she didn't trust her, like she thought Laurie was the one stalking her.

It was true, doubt remained, but the more she thought about it, the more unlikely it seemed Laurie was responsible for what was going on. Cally needed to see her, needed to *speak* to her. At least to say sorry. Even if Laurie didn't want to be friends any more. It must be hard enough anyway with all the rumours in the village about her arrest. Cally hadn't even thought about how that would have made Laurie feel.

Cally turned into Laurie's short drive and parked. Laurie's truck wasn't there, which made sense because Laurie was probably still at work.

Cally looked up at the first floor where Laurie's bedroom was. For a moment, she thought she saw someone looking down at her. It suddenly occurred to Cally that Laurie might have a girlfriend in there right now. Laurie hadn't mentioned that she was dating anybody, but it had been over a week since they'd last spoken.

Cally was suddenly embarrassed. What must the person think, looking down at a strange woman sitting in her car on the drive? Cally looked again and the person had gone, perhaps to call the police, or maybe the door would open any second and a pretty young woman would come over and politely ask what the fuck Cally was doing.

Cally started her car. She wasn't sure what she'd been thinking in the first place, turning up here. She put the car in reverse just as Laurie pulled into the drive.

Great. Perfect. She couldn't leave now. That was okay, though. She'd say she remembered she had something to do and needed to go.

Cally switched off the engine and got out of the car.

"Hey," she said as Laurie walked over with a slightly baffled look on her face. At least she wasn't angry.

"Hey. Everything all right?" Laurie asked. She had a rucksack slung over her back, and her jeans were dirty.

"Fine. I came over to speak to you—to apologise, really. I didn't realise you had a guest." Cally nodded towards Laurie's house.

The look of polite bafflement came back onto Laurie's face. "Guest? I don't have a guest. You want to come in?"

Laurie didn't wait for an answer. She walked past Cally and opened the front door.

"Don't you lock it?" Cally asked.

Laurie shrugged. "Sometimes. And sometimes I forget. I live in the middle of nowhere. And I have nothing worth stealing, anyway. Come on." Laurie held the door for Cally and waited for her to go in. "Do you want to talk right now, or do you mind if I get a quick shower first?" Laurie asked.

"No, I don't mind. Shower. If you want." Cally felt her cheeks heat. The last thing she wanted to think about was Laurie in the shower.

Laurie smiled like she knew exactly what was on Cally's mind. "Okay. Make yourself at home. You remember where the living room is."

Cally nodded and watched Laurie go upstairs. She went into the living room and looked at Laurie's bookshelves to give her something to do. It felt weird, being in here without Laurie.

Cally saw Jules's memoirs had been removed, and a dusty gap remained where the book had been. Cally was oddly touched. As she looked through the titles, she recognised a lot of them as books she'd read. Seemed like they had their tastes in books in common.

Cally heard the shower go on upstairs and tried to make her mind go somewhere else. On the mantelpiece were a collection of photos. Most of them featured Laurie with who Cally thought were family members. In one she stood in the forest with two older people who looked too much like her not to be her grandparents. Cally wondered if they lived in the village. Laurie hadn't mentioned them.

Another photo was of a man with his arm slung around Laurie's shoulder. The sea was behind them, and they both had sunglasses on. Cally smiled at the last picture in a silver frame. It was Laurie around three or four years old with the man from the other photo as he'd been as a boy. They were sitting on Santa's lap, one knee each. Laurie looked terrified, and the boy looked pretty unsure.

Cally picked up the photo to get a better look at it. Something resting behind it slid off the mantelpiece and onto the floor.

Another photo but this one without a frame. Laurie had obviously balanced it behind the frame. Cally's heart thumped and her skin prickled. She bent to pick it up.

"Everything okay?" Laurie asked from the doorway, and Cally nearly jumped out of her skin.

"Fucking Jesus Christ," Cally said and stood up quickly.

Laurie laughed and walked over. She bent quickly and picked up the photo. Put it in her pocket. "You okay? Sorry I made you jump."

Cally put her hand to her chest. "You nearly killed me."

"Because you were busy snooping," Laurie said but didn't seem to mind. She was smiling. She looked relaxed and amused, but Cally remembered the way she picked up the photo and smoothly put it in her pocket before Cally could see it. She wondered what it was of. Her suspicious mind wanted to wander off into suspicious territory, but she managed to stop it.

The photo could be of anything. An ex-girlfriend, an embarrassing school photo. Maybe of nothing interesting at all.

"I was looking at your photos, not snooping," Cally said. "They're on the mantelpiece. If I wanted to snoop, I would have gone upstairs."

Laurie laughed. "Rifled through my knicker drawer? Didn't have you down as one of those."

"Didn't have you down as someone with a knicker drawer," Cally shot back, and Laurie laughed.

"Do you want tea? Or something stronger?" Laurie asked.

"Tea is fine."

Cally followed Laurie into the kitchen. "We should talk about the other week."

Laurie put teabags in cups and filled the kettle. "Okay."

Cally could see Laurie wasn't going to be the one to start, which she guessed was fair enough. Cally was the one who came here, and Cally was the one who'd accused Laurie. She supposed she should be the one to start.

"I'm sorry."

"What for?" Laurie asked. Her voice was calm, but Cally could see she'd picked up a tea towel and was wringing it between her hands.

"For accusing you of maybe being my stalker," Cally said.

Laurie nodded. "Ah, yeah, that one stung."

"I know. I'm sorry," Cally said.

"But you don't *completely* trust that I'm not, do you?" Laurie asked.

Cally was surprised by the question. How should she answer? Be honest and risk alienating Laurie forever? In the end, her silence seemed to tell Laurie what she wanted to know.

"Look, Cally, I think I get it. You came out of a shitty relationship with someone who abused you. You thought you were shot of her, and then someone starts sending you poison-pen letters and standing outside your house in the night and breaking in. I'm trying hard to be understanding, but it's difficult," Laurie said.

Cally nodded. "I know. I *want* to not have any doubts. I just can't."

Laurie came to sit at the table. She passed Cally a mug of tea, then took her hand. "A big enough part of you must know it's not me, or you wouldn't have come here."

That took her aback. Cally hadn't thought about that. If she'd really believed it was Laurie, she wouldn't have come here, surely? Her brain ached with it all.

"I suppose I wouldn't," she said. "Laurie, I just can't *trust* myself. I don't know if the things I see or hear or feel are true any more."

"What do you mean?" Laurie asked.

"Like today, for instance. I could have *sworn* I saw someone in your upstairs window," Cally said.

"And you thought I was, what, hiding someone up there?" Laurie asked.

Cally laughed. "No. I thought you had…oh, I don't know."

"Yes, you do."

Cally sighed and braced herself to feel mortified. "It occurred to me that maybe you had a girlfriend in here, and I nearly left."

Laurie grinned. Then she laughed. "A girlfriend? Really? And you didn't like that?"

"Oh, shut up. You don't have to look so pleased with yourself."

"I'm just surprised you care," Laurie said.

Cally looked at her. "This is why I feel so…so *fucked up*. Like I can't trust myself. I have all these suspicions and all these fears and at the same time—"

"You fancy me," Laurie said.

Cally shoved Laurie's shoulder lightly. "I do *not*."

"Yes, you do. It's okay, though. Because I fancy you too," Laurie said.

"Even now?" Cally asked. Something inside her shifted. She hadn't felt it in a long time, but she knew instantly it was lust, and that was a relief when she hadn't known anything but dread for such a long time.

Laurie nodded. "Even now, after you've had me arrested and blatantly called me a stalker." Laurie frowned. "Maybe we're both fucked up."

Cally laughed. "We must be because that takes the whole *treat 'em mean, keep 'em keen* to a whole new level."

"So, what do you want to do about it?" Laurie asked.

Cally's stomach dropped. What did she want to do about it? That was an easy answer. What she *should* do about it was something altogether different. If she was being sensible, she'd tell Laurie she wasn't in a position to *do* anything about the way she felt. Instead, she leaned forward and kissed her.

For a second, Laurie didn't respond, and Cally was pleased she'd surprised her. She quickly got over it and kissed Cally back in a way that made her toes curl.

Cally was the first one to break the kiss. She meant to say they should stop there, that they shouldn't have done even that. Instead, she stood up and took Laurie's hand.

"Take me to bed," Cally said.

Laurie stood up so fast she nearly knocked the chair over. She recovered herself and led Cally upstairs.

Chapter Thirty-six

The bed was as comfortable as it looked. Laurie laid her down gently and then stretched out on top of her.

Cally spread her legs and felt the seam of her jeans pull tight across her centre. As Laurie moved above her, kissing her face, her neck, her chest, the seam of Cally's jeans rubbed against her.

She reached up and linked her arms behind Laurie's head, pulling their mouths back together. The kisses became hungrier and more frantic, and Cally started to move against Laurie as Laurie pushed against her.

Laurie reached under Cally's top and stroked along her side. She ran one finger along the waistband of Cally's jeans, making her shiver.

Laurie's hand moved up to her bra, and she gently cupped one breast and squeezed. Cally gasped as the sensation fired down her body and straight to the centre of her.

It was all the encouragement Laurie needed. With a rough efficiency, she pulled Cally's top off and unhooked her bra. She'd barely pushed it away before her mouth was on Cally's breast, sucking and licking and pulling gently.

Cally groaned and begged Laurie for more. Laurie obliged. She reached down and unzipped Cally's jeans. Cally helped Laurie pull them off.

Now she was almost naked, while Laurie was still fully clothed. The power imbalance should have bothered, her but instead it turned her on more. The feel of Laurie's soft cotton joggers against her bare legs made her ache.

"Please," Cally moaned. She wasn't sure what she was asking for until Laurie's mouth found her centre, and then she realised that's what she'd been asking for all along.

She spread her legs as wide as she could and reached down to touch Laurie's head. Cally moved her where she wanted her and cried out when Laurie found the perfect rhythm and stroke.

Cally bucked and ground her hips and pushed herself into Laurie's mouth. She felt her orgasm begin to build and gripped Laurie's head tight. Then, she was coming. She arched her back and cried out.

Before her orgasm had fully finished, Laurie flipped Cally onto her front, grabbed her hips, and pulled her back and up onto all fours. She pushed two fingers deep inside Cally and began to pump hard. The sensation of it and the unexpectedness forced Cally into another climax. She pushed back hard onto Laurie's fingers over and over again, milking everything out of her orgasm.

Finally, Cally collapsed onto the bed and Laurie fell down beside her.

"Bloody hell," Laurie managed.

Cally couldn't speak. Her limbs were weak and watery, and a pleasant hum worked its way through her body. For the first time in forever, she felt peaceful and relaxed.

Beside her, Laurie pushed herself up onto her side. She trailed one hand along Cally's ribcage, down to her belly button, and along her hip bones. The intimacy of it wasn't unwelcome, and that surprised Cally.

"You okay?" Laurie asked.

"Better than," Cally answered. She shifted a little so she was facing Laurie. "How are you?"

Laurie grinned and kissed the tip of Cally's nose. "I'm actually pretty good myself, thanks."

"Really?" Cally asked. She let her hand drift down to Laurie's joggers and tugged on them gently. "Do you think you could be better than pretty good?"

"Depends on what you had in mind," Laurie replied.

Cally was enjoying the game. Instead of answering, she leaned over and kissed Laurie deeply. She slipped her hand inside Laurie's joggers and was pleased to find Laurie wasn't all right at all. She was soaking wet. "Want me to do something about this?" Cally asked.

Laurie broke the kiss for a moment. "Only if you don't mind," she said and made Cally laugh.

She definitely didn't mind.

Cally teased Laurie with her fingers for a while until Laurie begged her to put her mouth on her. Cally slid down the bed and obliged. She worked her slowly, made Laurie writhe and curse. Eventually, she gave Laurie what she wanted. Cally licked and sucked Laurie until she exploded in her mouth.

For a moment, Laurie lay there without moving. She didn't speak, either.

"Laurie?" Cally leaned over her and touched her face. "Laurie, are you okay?"

Suddenly, Laurie reached up pulled Cally towards her and rolled her onto her back so Laurie was lying on top of her. Cally couldn't help it—she squealed.

"I can't believe you did that." Cally pushed at Laurie's shoulder half-heartedly. "That was mean."

Laurie laughed and kissed the tip of Cally's nose again. "You loved it."

"I bloody didn't. Who does something like that after sex?" Cally asked.

"The same someone who's going to go downstairs and get you a nice cold glass of water." Laurie rolled off her, off the bed, and into a standing position in a neat move Cally was sure she'd practised. She rolled her eyes.

"I am thirsty," Cally said.

"And some snacks."

"Snacks?" Cally asked, forgetting to be mad.

Laurie nodded. "Yeah, snacks. You want snacks?" She walked towards the bedroom door.

"I want snacks," Cally said, then shouted after her, "the good ones, not the crap you have leftover from Christmas."

She heard Laurie laughing as she went down the stairs.

CHAPTER THIRTY-SEVEN

Cally woke with a start and, for a second, panicked when she felt another person's arm draped over her. Her first thought was that leaving Jules had all been a dream and she was lying next to her, back in the nightmare.

Cally lifted the arm off her and turned her head. When she saw a mop of dark hair covering most of the face lying next to her, relief suffused her. It was just Laurie. Laurie who she'd had sex with. More than once.

Really good sex.

Great sex, in fact.

Cally sat up and tried to work out how she felt about it. She attempted to summon some regret, though she wasn't sure why. None would come. She probed the thought that this was a bad idea and couldn't find the will to actually believe that. She liked Laurie. They had amazing sex. Laurie was easy-going and laid back. Even in the beginning, Jules had never been that. Their relationship was intense from the start, and Cally quickly worked out Jules didn't have much of a sense of boundaries. That alone should have been a red flag, but it wasn't.

Cally sighed. She hadn't seen any red flags from Laurie yet. It didn't mean they weren't there, but they hadn't exactly known each other long enough for Cally to find out. Plus, there was the little matter of the stalker. And the fact Cally had come over because it wasn't all that long ago she was accusing Laurie of stalking.

And that was the crux of it, wasn't it? Could she continue to sleep with someone she didn't trust? And did she definitely not trust Laurie? Lots of questions.

Cally thought back to the photo Laurie put in her pocket. The one that fell to the floor when Cally picked up the photo of Laurie and her brother. It was probably still in Laurie's joggers. They'd gone from down there to up here and been together since. When Laurie went downstairs for snacks—really great snacks, actually—she hadn't been wearing any clothes.

Cally sat up slowly in Laurie's bed. Laurie didn't stir. She carefully pushed the covers off herself and put her feet on the floor.

Feeling guilty and sly about it didn't stop her from creeping over to where Laurie had thrown her joggers. Feeling sneaky and shifty didn't stop her from picking them up.

"What are you doing?" Laurie asked.

Cally jumped and spun around. "Fuck. You nearly gave me a heart attack. I was trying not to wake you."

Laurie got out of bed and took her joggers from Cally. "What are you doing, Cally?"

Cally thought quickly. "I was cold. I thought sleeping in these would be more comfortable."

"Oh," Laurie said.

"What did you think I was doing?" Cally asked, feeling like a complete piece of shit for lying.

"I thought…never mind. It doesn't matter. I'll get you some pyjamas instead. These will be much too warm," Laurie said.

Cally nodded, and even though she'd lied, she couldn't help wondering if Laurie was stopping her from looking at the photo on purpose. And how quickly had she woken up? Had she been asleep at all?

Cally made herself stop. She'd just had sex with the woman, for fuck's sake. They'd been asleep in the same bed for hours, and Laurie hadn't tried to kill her yet. Maybe she didn't want Cally to see the photo because it wasn't any of Cally's business. It didn't mean she was hiding something, did it?

"Everything okay?" Laurie asked. She held out a pair of cotton pyjama bottoms and a T-shirt.

"Yes, fine," Cally said.

"Really? Because if you're panicking about what happened, or you're feeling weird, it's cool if you wanted to leave," Laurie said.

Cally smiled. How could someone so lovely be a stalker? The same way Jules ended up being a complete fucker, she supposed. "I'm not panicking. I just…it's been a while since I shared a bed with a woman."

Laurie smiled. "I know what you mean. I really won't be offended if you want to go home, though."

"I never pump and dump," Cally said.

Laurie snorted. "Cally, that's fucking gross."

"Sorry."

Laurie shook her head and grinned. "No idea you were so vulgar."

"There's a lot you don't know about me," Cally said.

The grin left Laurie's face, and she stepped towards Cally. Gently, she cupped Cally's face. "I know. I'm kind of hoping you'll let me find out. And for now, I'm happy to do that on your terms." Laurie kissed Cally's lips softly.

"That was really smooth," Cally said.

Laurie took a mock bow. "Thank you. I've been working on being suave."

"It's paying off."

Laurie laughed. "Let's get back into bed—it's bloody freezing." Laurie pulled another pair of pyjama bottoms and a T-shirt out of the drawer and put them on.

When they were back in bed, side by side, Cally said, "I don't know that I've much to offer you at the moment."

Laurie was silent for a few seconds, and Cally worried she'd offended her. Instead, Laurie reached for Cally's hand. "I meant what I said. I'm happy to do things on your terms for now. But just so you know, there will reach a point when I'll want more from you. It's just how I am. I can't do casual for long if I really like someone."

"You really like me?" Cally asked.

"I'm getting there."

"I think I'd like to give you more—in time. I just don't know if I can any more," Cally admitted.

"She really fucked you up, didn't she?"

Cally nodded and was annoyed with herself when she felt tears prickle her eyes. "Yes. And I don't know if I want to take a chance again. It's not personal."

"I know. It's so strange. She seemed so *nice* on the telly. I guess you can't ever tell about a person."

"No, you can't," Cally said.

"Which is why I'm not offended you don't trust me yet. I'm confident you will, though. In time."

"I really want you to be right," Cally said. She'd managed to force the tears back down. Now, she just felt sad.

"What do you want, Cally?" Laurie asked. "If you could have anything in the world?"

Cally smiled. "I'd like to have met you earlier, I think. What do you want?"

"It's pretty boring really. I want what my parents have. To get married and have kids and live in my house with my garden and bake bread and work in the forest. Probably nothing like what you want."

"Why do you think that? I moved out here too, didn't I?" Cally said.

"I suppose you did."

"And I would have loved kids. Jules just never…it doesn't matter."

"She didn't want them?" Laurie asked.

"No, she didn't. I think she didn't want the focus off her. And I'm bloody glad we didn't bring kids into that shitshow of a marriage."

Laurie didn't say anything else. Cally guessed there was nothing really to say. They lay there for a while longer, holding hands. It was nice.

Cally thought Laurie must have fallen back to sleep, but then Laurie said, very quietly, "I wish I'd met you before too. I really wish that. Things could have been so different."

CHAPTER THIRTY-EIGHT

The first thing Cally did when she got home the next morning was go down to the cabins to feed the dog. The pup was waiting for her, as she'd starting doing the last few mornings. Cally felt a rush when the dog stood up and wagged her tail and grinned a doggy grin.

"Hey, girl," Cally said. "Hey, baby. You hungry?"

The dog turned in a circle and Cally laughed. "Who taught you that, then? You're a clever girl."

Cally held out the bowl of food and the dog licked her lips.

"Let's try something different today. After you've eaten, let's see if you'll come up to the house with me."

Cally put the food down, and the dog came over and starting chomping it down. Cally was satisfied to see she'd put on weight. She still wasn't anywhere near what she should be, but the dull skeletal look had gone. She still needed to see a vet, though.

When the dog finished eating—which took about five seconds—Cally picked up the bowl. She stepped back and patted her thigh with her free hand. "Come on, girl, come here."

The dog took a step towards her, then stopped and cocked her head at Cally.

"What's up? Don't you want to come with me and live in my nice warm house?"

The dog's head turned to the right. She was completely oblivious to Cally now. The dog growled low in her throat. She moved to the right so that she was standing between Cally and the trees. She growled low again in her throat.

"What is it?" Cally asked the dog—as if she'd answer. Besides, it was pretty obvious what was going on. Something was in the wood, and the dog didn't like it. Cally shivered.

The dog started to bark low and savage, and far from being scared, Cally felt safer. Thin as the dog was, Cally didn't think anyone would want to go up against her. Not with those teeth.

Suddenly, the dog bolted into the trees and was gone.

"Fuck," Cally said. She decided not to hang around and went back up to the house. The chances of it being the figure in orange were low, considering she'd put up cameras on the cabins. Most likely, the dog had seen or heard a fox and was defending her territory. Regardless, Cally wasn't an idiot.

The first thing she saw when she opened the front door was the letter lying innocently on the doormat. Except Cally knew there was nothing innocent about it.

Like the day before, she picked it up by the corner and used a letter opener to slit it open. Cally opened the folded white paper. Typed neatly in the middle, it said: *12 because you shouldn't have done that.*

It didn't take a genius to figure it out. This was some kind of countdown, and Cally had pissed off the stalker who'd deducted a further day or week or month or fucking century—who knew?

Cally resisted the urge to rip the stupid letter into tiny pieces and stomp it into the ground. Shouldn't have done *what*? Slept with Laurie was the only thing she could think of. Which meant the stalker was living up to their name and doing a fantastic job of keeping tabs on her. Not that *that* would have been rocket science either. They knew what her car looked like and had probably driven past Laurie's house and seen it parked there last night. And probably again this morning.

Cally dug out the business card from her bag and called the detective in charge of her case.

She ended the call with the detective feeling even more frustrated. She knew the police were doing everything they could. They'd installed a panic alarm at the house, did drive-bys each night, and were working hard on the letters. But no one still had any idea who the stalker was.

In a village so small, surely *someone* had seen them? They had to be hanging around to be able to watch her and know her movements. But then, a lot of tourists passed through, and they always went into the village. The stalker could easily pass for one of them if they wanted to.

Cally had said she'd go down to the pub tonight. Maybe she

could ask around there. According to Sian, everyone already knew her business anyway, so she might as well ask.

Before the stupid letter, Cally had been looking forward to a night out, especially now she knew Laurie was going this time. Maybe she should just focus on that instead and let the police do their job.

Chapter Thirty-nine

The pub was exactly the same as when she'd come in last time—same faces, same noisy packed interior, same band setting up over by the dance floor. Cally smiled. She felt good. A couple of locals came up to her, and even though she braced herself for questions about what happened the other week, none came. There was polite interest in the work going on up at Five Oaks and general queries about how she was.

The same butcher offered to buy her a drink, but she bought him one instead. Cally took his number and promised she'd call in the week to set something up so they could talk about him supplying her guests.

She shuffled her way over towards the dance floor. All the tables were taken, but there was a long thin shelf along one wall where she could put her drink down and observe. Cally watched people greet each other and tables of families or friends laughing.

"Cally," called the woman from the grocery shop, "come over here—there's a spare seat."

Cally went over and tried to remember the names of the people she was introduced to—the grocery woman was Barbara, and her friends were Pam, Clive, Pete, and Sheila. All in their early sixties and couples by the looks of it. She sat with them.

"Colin tells me you came up from London. Colin's my son—the butcher," Sheila said.

"Yes, I did. And I'd never go back in a million years."

The table nodded, pleased with her answer. Cally felt like a bit of a suck-up, but she told herself she was networking. She needed these people to like her. The truth was, she *wanted* them to like her. Cally wanted to be part of something. The community in Halesbrook was a good one.

"So, what's happening with Laurie, then? Your car was seen up at hers last night." Pam waggled her eyebrows. Cally felt herself go red, and Barbara nudged Pam.

"Pam, leave her alone."

"What? Why? It's the best bit of gossip for months. Don't worry, Cally, most of us are very open-minded. And we've known Laurie since she was a baby. There's a few old-fashioned people in the village. You just ignore them, though." Pam patted her hand, and Cally laughed.

"Laurie and I are friends," she said.

Sheila rolled her eyes. "Friends. *Sure*."

"Leave her alone, or she'll think we're all gossips," Barbara said.

"It's okay, nothing wrong with a bit of gossip." And then because she was feeling brave and happy and relaxed, she added, "Laurie and I are *special* friends," then winked at Pam and Barbara and Sheila.

They burst into laughter, and Pam pulled Cally into a hug. "Oh, I do like you."

"Can anyone join or is it pensioners only?" Laurie asked from behind them.

"You cheeky little sod," Barbara said. "I don't know where you get it from. Get a round in, for your insolence."

"The whole table?" Laurie said. "Mum, that'll cost me a fortune."

Cally did a double take. Laurie's *mum*? Oh God, no.

"I don't care. Buy one for your dad too—he's over by the pool table," Barbara said.

Laurie bent and kissed Barbara on the cheek. She winked at Cally, then left for the bar.

"Barbara, I had no idea—" Cally started to say.

Barbara waved Cally away. "Don't be silly. You've nothing to feel embarrassed about. I should have told you who I was. While I'm at it, Pam and Sheila are her aunts, Clive and Pete are her uncles, and her dad, Joe, is over by the pool table with her brother, sister, and cousins." Barbara sat back, looking pleased with herself.

Cally wasn't sure what to say. "That's…nice."

Sheila laughed. "It's a lot. Sorry, love."

"No, no, it's fine. I just didn't realise you were all related," Cally said.

"Why would you? And I don't want you thinking Laurie set this up—she didn't," Barbara said. "I just liked you so much at the planning meeting, and I've been wanting to talk to you for ages. I didn't know until Pam told me about your car at Laurie's that you were even friends."

"It's really okay. I'm having a good time," Cally said. She meant it too. Laurie's family were lovely. She wished she hadn't told them she and Laurie were sleeping together, but you couldn't have everything. And they seemed to take it well, so there was that.

"Right, I found Dad and gave him and the rest of them their drinks. Here's yours." Laurie plonked a tray down on the table.

"Good girl," Shelia said and patted Laurie's cheek when she bent over.

Laurie rolled her eyes at Cally who laughed. "And here's yours. I got you vodka and tonic. Colin said that's what you drank."

"Thanks," Cally said, suddenly feeling shy. She could feel Laurie's whole family watching them, and Laurie was oblivious.

"What?" Laurie asked, seeing all eyes on her and Cally.

"Nothing, love," Barbara said. "Thanks for the drinks."

"Right," Laurie replied. "How have you been?" Laurie asked Cally.

"Since last night," Clive said.

"And this morning," Pete called from the other side of the table, and everyone laughed.

Cally saw Laurie go bright red. Cally mouthed *sorry* to Laurie, who looked confused.

"Right, that's enough. Leave them alone," Barbara said. "Let's go up for a dance."

"The music hasn't started yet," Sheila said.

"Shut up, Sheila," Pam said, and they all got up en masse and went to the dance floor.

"Oh, Laurie, I'm so sorry," Cally said. "I didn't know you were related to them. They asked about my car in your drive this morning, and I said we were special friends." Cally waited for Laurie to explode with anger for embarrassing her.

Instead, she burst out laughing. "Those nosy old bastards. They did it on purpose, you know. Waited until you'd dished before they told you who they were. Well, *they're* buying us drinks all night."

"Thanks for not being mad at me," Cally said.

"Mad? Why would I be mad at you?" Laurie asked. Her face clouded over—now she did look mad. "Cally, there's nothing for me to be mad about. That wouldn't be a reasonable response."

Now Cally was embarrassed. It was so difficult trying to readjust her thinking, trying to remember who she used to be before Jules fucked her up. This was why she didn't want a relationship. It was hard enough trying to readjust to life as an autonomous human being. Adding someone else to the mix was asking for trouble.

"Hey—Cally." Laurie gently took Cally's face in her hand. "Stop overthinking. Everything is okay. My family are sneaky fuckers and always have been. Drink your drink and then we'll dance and have a good night."

Cally looked at Laurie. Her eyes were kind and unguarded. "You make it sound easy."

"It is," Laurie said, "if you let it be."

Cally nodded. If she let it be. Well, she'd try it. She had nothing to lose, after all.

CHAPTER FORTY

As it turned out, it really was that easy. Cally had a few more drinks courtesy of Laurie's family and danced to almost every song. When she wasn't dancing, she was laughing. Cally couldn't remember ever having such a good night.

She danced with Pam and Sheila and Barbara and Clive and Pete and a whole load of Laurie's cousins and siblings. Every time she sat down, another relative would either push a drink into her hand or pull her up onto the dance floor.

Laurie seemed happy to sit back and watch her have a good time. She laughed when Clive dipped Cally low on the dance floor, or when Pam jokingly pulled her close on a slow number. Cally tried hard not to like Laurie more than she already did, but she was making it difficult.

Cally tried to imagine Jules in this scenario and couldn't. First, there was no way Jules would leave London unless it was for the money on a job. Plus, she liked quiet fancy restaurants and trendy bars. A local pub that smelled of stale beer and wasn't filled with Insta-ready people would have been her idea of a shitty time.

Cally loved it.

And she loved the way Laurie was so at home here. With Laurie, there was no pretence. Jules had always given off this alpha energy, and Cally knew it was only to cover her many insecurities. Laurie was truly comfortable in her own skin. It was obvious in the way she laughed and hugged and didn't bat an eye when Cally danced with everyone but her.

The band struck up another song and told the crowd it would be their last. Cally couldn't let the evening end without dancing with

Laurie one last time. She declined Colin's invitation and reached out for Laurie's hand. "Dance with me?" she asked, feeling shy.

Laurie smiled and let Cally lead her to the dance floor.

They moved close together as the guitarist plucked the melody of a well-known love song. The lead singer didn't do a bad job of it, either.

Laurie's arms came around Cally's waist and held her gently. Cally leaned in close and let Laurie lead.

"This is nice," Laurie said in her ear.

"It is," Cally agreed.

"Is it too soon to have another sleepover?" Laurie asked.

Cally leaned back in Laurie's arms. "Well, it is Friday night. And I am quite tipsy."

Laurie frowned. "How tipsy? Too tipsy for a sleepover?"

Cally linked her arms around Laurie's neck and pulled her closer. "No. Not too tipsy for that."

"Sure? Because if you are—"

Cally kissed her and that shut her up. She was definitely tipsy because she never would have kissed Laurie in a pub full of people sober.

"Wow," Laurie said when Cally broke away.

"Did your family see that?" Cally asked.

Laurie looked over Cally's shoulder. "Yep. And now they're all gossiping about it."

"Good," Cally said, and Laurie laughed and spun her.

Laurie's uncle Pete dropped them home to Cally's and laughed when Laurie shot them a middle finger as they drove away making kissing noises.

"Come on, let's go in," Cally said. Despite the blazing security lights, she didn't feel safe outside her house any more. She didn't really feel safe inside it, either. Maybe coming back here was a mistake. They should have gone to Laurie's.

"Come on." Laurie embraced Cally from behind and walked her to the front door. "Let's get inside, so I can ravish you."

Cally couldn't help but laugh. "Ravish me? How old are you?"

"Says you. When I came in the pub you were sitting with the cast of *Cocoon*."

"Laurie! That's your family." Cally giggled.

Giggled? Who *was* she? Cally didn't think she'd giggled since she was a child.

She unlocked the multitude of locks and pushed open the door with Laurie still stuck to her back.

Cally was relieved to see the thermostat was in the same position she'd left it earlier. She punched in the alarm code, making sure to shield it from Laurie and feeling bad all the same.

Laurie didn't seem to mind—she was already waiting on the stairs.

"You're keen," Cally said.

"Of course I am. I've been waiting all day to do things to you." Laurie waggled her eyebrows.

"Do things to me? That sounds sexy and sinister at the same time." Cally walked to her.

"Because I am both sexy and sinister," Laurie said, holding out her arms.

Cally laughed—she didn't remember laughing with anyone as much as she laughed with Laurie. "You are definitely not sinister." She let Laurie pull her up the stairs.

"Just sexy, then. Which way's the bedroom?" Laurie asked.

"Go left," Cally said.

Laurie pushed open Cally's bedroom door and pulled Cally in. "If you need to puke, now's the time. Before we get going."

Cally shoved Laurie playfully. "Sexy *and* romantic. I don't need to puke."

"Okay, good." Laurie walked Cally to the bed and pushed her down gently. "Prepare to be sexually satisfied."

Cally giggled again. She really needed to stop doing that. She pulled Laurie down on top of her. "I can't wait."

CHAPTER FORTY-ONE

The blaring alarm reached her in her dream. She was on a beach and the sound was so out of place. As she came up out of sleep, Cally heard it for what it was.

Her burglar alarm.

Fuck, how long had it been going off? Cally was instantly awake and alert. She jumped up and reached for the panic alarm by her bed. She pushed the button and prayed it worked. In theory, it should bring police units rushing to her house.

She looked over to where Laurie had been sleeping and saw she was gone. Cally's heart thumped in her chest. Where was she? Cally called out her name. No answer.

She pulled on her dressing gown and ran out of the bedroom. She could see from the landing the front door stood wide open. Who had opened it? Laurie? Or someone else?

Terrified for Laurie, Cally ran downstairs. She called her name again, and still Laurie didn't answer. The smell hit her when she got to the front door. She probably would have smelled it sooner if not for the panic.

Burning.

Dear Jesus, something was burning. Cally stepped outside and immediately saw it was the wood. *Her* wood was burning.

Barefoot, she ran across the drive barely feeling the gravel dig into her feet and cut them. She flew across the field and to the edge of the wood. She called out Laurie's name again, certain now where she was.

Icy fear gripped her, and terrible thoughts tried to force their way in. Cally pushed them back and went into the wood. What she'd first thought was the wood on fire, she now realised were the cabins. All of them.

Cally heard the distant wail of sirens and knew the police were on their way. But where was Laurie?

Cally walked further into the wood. She was almost at the last cabin before she saw her. She was dragging something out of the door of a cabin. The flames raged behind her, and Cally ran to her.

When she was metres away, she realised Laurie had the dog, and she was pulling her away from the fire.

"What are you doing?" Cally asked.

"What does it look like? Help me," Laurie snapped. "I didn't know she was in there. I didn't know."

Cally wasn't sure what Laurie meant by that, but for now she picked up the back end of the dog and helped Laurie carry her away from the flames.

"What were you thinking, Laurie? You could have been killed," Cally said as they reached the edge of the wood and put the dog down. Behind them, police cars and—thank God—a fire engine were racing towards them.

Cally bent down near the dog. She was still breathing. "Help me. We need to take her to a vet."

Laurie pulled her phone out from her jeans pocket and dialled. "I'll call my uncle to take us. I can't drive—I've had too much to drink."

Laurie spoke briefly to her uncle, and by the time she hung up, police officers and firefighters were running towards them.

The good news was the fire didn't spread to the trees. Laurie had poured water on the ground around several of the cabins before realising the dog was inside one of them.

The bad news was Cally and Laurie now sat under harsh fluorescent lights in the vet's waiting room while the vet tried to save the dog.

She'd inhaled a lot of smoke before Laurie managed to pull her out, and she had some burns on her paw pads. Poor thing must have been terrified. Cally couldn't understand someone who would do something like this. The stalker was ramping up. She wasn't sure what that meant for Five Oaks, but she couldn't think about that now. Now she waited for news on the dog.

"You can't keep calling her *the dog*, you know," Laurie said.

"Huh?" Cally wasn't really listening.

"She needs a name," Laurie explained.

"I don't know if naming her now is such a good idea."

"Why not? She deserves a name." Laurie's voice cracked on *name*, and Cally reached for her hand.

"You're right. We should name her," Cally said.

"We? No, she's your dog." Laurie shook her head.

"You saved her. If it wasn't for you, she would have died in there," Cally said.

"She would have gotten out sooner if I hadn't been so concerned about the fucking trees," Laurie said.

"You didn't know she was in there," Cally said.

"I should have. You *told* me you had a dog living in one of the cabins," Laurie said.

Cally didn't know what to say to make her feel better. Then she remembered what Laurie said when she found her pulling the dog out of the cabin. It had seemed strange for Laurie to say she didn't know the dog was in there. She'd sounded…regretful. All Cally's old fears of Laurie being the stalker had resurfaced, but she hadn't had time to dwell on them.

Now, though, Cally wondered how Laurie had got to the cabins so fast.

"Laurie, how did you know the cabins were on fire?" Cally asked.

"I got up for a drink. I saw the flames from the window," Laurie said.

It made sense. Sounded completely believable.

"And it was you who set the alarm off?"

"I didn't know the code. I just opened the door and ran," Laurie said.

"And I got up pretty soon after that. So you had maybe three minutes on me?" Cally said.

Laurie sighed. "Cally, if you want to do some more investigations into whether I'm your stalker, that's fine. Can we just wait until we know about the dog, please?"

"I wasn't—"

"Yes, you were."

She was. What was wrong with her? Everything inside her told her Laurie wasn't the one doing it. But still, she couldn't seem to stop accusing her. And actually, it was only after they had sex that Cally stopped thinking it might be Laurie. And even then, she was still suspicious. That photo…

The door to the waiting room opened, and the vet walked in. She and Laurie both stood up. Cally tried to judge from the vet's expression whether the news would be good or bad.

"She's doing okay," the vet said quickly, and Cally heard Laurie's deep sigh of relief.

"Thank you," Cally said.

"She's a fighter. There was a lot of smoke inhalation, but there's no damage to her internal organs. Just some severe smoke inhalation and the burns to her feet."

"But she'll be okay?" Cally asked.

The vet nodded and smiled. "Looks that way. I want to keep her in for a couple of days, though."

"Sure," Laurie said.

"You said she was a stray. Am I calling the council to take her?" the vet asked.

"No," Cally said quickly. "I'm keeping her. If that's allowed?"

The vet laughed. "It's allowed. She'll need to be microchipped, though. Before you take her home, I can give her all her injections."

"Okay. Thanks," Cally said, relieved.

"Well, you should both go home and get some sleep. I'll call you tomorrow with an update. And you should probably think of a name for her," the vet said.

"We will," Cally replied.

Laurie called her poor uncle to come back out and get them. Cally would have to get him something to say thank you.

"Do you want to come back to mine, or are you worried I might kill you in your sleep?" Laurie asked as they waited in the car park for their lift.

"That's not funny," Cally said.

Laurie sighed. "You're right. It's not. I'm sorry."

"It's okay. I get why you're pissed off. Can't be fun to keep being questioned," Cally said.

"You've just had your business burned to the ground. I think I can forgive you," Laurie said.

"Thanks."

"I wasn't going to say anything until it's finalised, but the forestry commission aren't moving ahead with trying to reverse the planning decision," Laurie said. "I know that's probably cold comfort after what happened, but—"

"Thank you. It's good. I'm pleased," Cally said, trying to feel pleased.

"I'm really sorry, Cally. About what happened. I can't begin to imagine what it's like for you," Laurie said.

Cally leaned against Laurie, who wrapped her arms around Cally as Cally started to cry.

CHAPTER FORTY-TWO

Joe and Phil made all sorts of noises as they looked at the wreckage of the cabins from behind the police tape. Whistles and teeth sucking and groans. Cally knew from the noises alone it wasn't good news.

"None of them can be saved," Phil said.

"Probably cheaper to knock them down and start again anyway," Joe added.

"How can you tell from here?" Cally asked.

"You said these at the front were in the best shape. And they aren't salvageable," Joe said.

He made a good point. Cally was tired and irritable. The fire investigation woman was still looking around and probably wouldn't release the scene for another few days yet. The police had copied all of the CCTV footage from that night, and they were crawling all over the village talking to people and looking for any other footage that might have caught the arsonist.

The assumption was that it was the stalker who did it. Like clockwork, Cally received a letter this morning from them. *11* was typed on a single piece of paper, just like the others. No extra little note with another deduction like yesterday. Cally guessed that, whoever they were, they agreed burning her cabins to the ground was enough.

She'd left Laurie's this morning first thing. So much for a lazy Saturday. When she thought back to last night at the pub, Cally was angry. She'd had such a good night, the best night in years. Now it was ruined, the whole memory of it tainted. She supposed that was the plan. If the stalker had followed her to Laurie's house yesterday, then it was no big stretch to think they'd probably been in the pub last night too.

Maybe the sight of Cally having such a good time was more than they could bear. The quickest way to change it was to do something like this.

That theory reminded Cally of Jules. The way she would try to destroy anything good Cally had. If she was in a good mood, Jules would make sure she was back to being anxious and miserable in no time. The stalker wasn't any different in that respect.

Cally sighed. What was she going to do now? If she started on the cabins and the stalker burned them down again… She supposed she'd have to hire a security guard or something. The police wanted her to move out of the house and go somewhere else completely. How was she going to do that? Plus, with all the money she'd spent on security, the safest place for her was *in* her house.

Last night, the stalker had to make do with destroying the cabins. Since she'd installed security, they hadn't been able to do more than stand in the trees outside and watch. Cally wondered if it infuriated them that they couldn't get inside any more.

She walked Joe and Phil back to their van and thanked them for coming out on a Saturday. She'd have a think over the weekend about whether she definitely wanted to start demolition on the cabins.

She had enough money to delay the build for a bit longer, but who knew when the stalker was going to get caught. She couldn't shut herself away in her house forever—she refused to do that. And she didn't want to sell up and move away. She was starting to make a life here. She didn't want to lose that.

As she walked back up to the house, her phone buzzed, dragging her out of her own head. She looked at the screen and was surprised to see it was Sian. The message was brief, but it was a start at least. Sian told her she'd heard about the cabins and was sorry. She asked if Cally was okay and asked if there was anything she could do to help.

Cally texted back that she could bring over a bottle of wine later if she wanted. Cally waited while the three dots that indicated someone was typing shimmered on the screen. Relief washed over her when Sian replied she'd be by as soon as she closed the bakery at two.

That gave Cally enough time to get to the vet's to see the dog—she really had to give her a name—and back, in time for Sian to come over. The idea of spending the afternoon drinking wine appealed to her. And it would be good for her and Laurie not to see each other for a few days. Cally didn't want *that* particular situation getting out of hand to the point they were seeing each other every day.

Cally went into the house feeling better than she had when she woke up this morning.

CHAPTER FORTY-THREE

Cally had a sense of déjà vu. She put two bottles of wine in the fridge and turned on the oven to preheat. Part of her waited for her phone to ping with an alert to say someone had activated a camera outside. As she walked around the house tidying up, she glanced out of every window, thinking she would see the figure in orange standing out there, looking in.

Cally told herself to stop. She wanted to enjoy the evening. She didn't want the stalker to ruin everything, though God knew they were trying.

Because that was really what it came down to.

Whoever they were, they hated the life she was making for herself. They hated that she was happy. That's why they'd tried to burn the cabins down. Cally couldn't think of one person who hated her enough to do something like that—she couldn't think of one person who hated her, full stop.

The only person she could think of that could harbour that much hate for her was Jules. And Jules was dead. She *was* dead. They hadn't found a body, but no one could survive a fall from a cliff like that.

A little voice in the back of Cally's mind whispered, *But* did *she fall?*

Of course she did.

Why would she fake something like that? It's true, she was about to be arrested and dragged through the courts. And all her endorsements and TV gigs dropped her like a hot potato when the news broke. But how would pretending to kill herself help? She had no money, nowhere to go. And it wasn't like the UK was America. Someone would have spotted her. The country was too small to disappear in for long.

The only reason Jules would do something like that would be to… to hurt Cally. But that couldn't be it, could it?

The doorbell rang and made Cally jump. She opened the app on her phone and saw Sian standing there on the doorstep clutching a carrier bag. It looked heavy. Cally groaned inwardly. She was going to have such a hangover in the morning.

Cally opened the door. "Hey, Sian."

Sian grabbed Cally and pulled her into a hug. "I'm sorry I've been such a cow."

"Don't be silly. I started it, anyway," Cally said.

Sian walked inside and thrust the bag at Cally. "Here. Peace offering. I reckon we'll drink all of it tonight."

Cally took the bag and went into the kitchen to pour some wine and put the pizza on. "How have you been?" she asked. She took Sian's wine bottles out of the bag and put them in the fridge. Looked like Sian had already started on one of them.

"Not bad. Feeling a bit shit for ignoring you, selling lots of sticky buns and bacon rolls, you know," Sian said and took the glass of wine Cally offered her. "I'm so sorry about your cabins."

"Thanks," Cally said. "It was pretty bad."

Sian rubbed Cally's arm. "Thank God Laurie was here."

Cally nodded. "It would have been a lot worse otherwise. We caught it quick."

"Can you fix them?" Sian asked and took a big gulp of wine.

"No, but we saved the woods. And the dog," Cally said.

"Oh yes, the dog." Sian held out her glass for a top up. "Have you tamed the beast yet?"

Cally poured Sian another glass and drank some more of her own wine to try to catch up. "We were definitely getting there. I'm not sure how she'll be after what happened, though. I'll have to keep her indoors while she recovers too."

"So, you are keeping her—I knew you would," Sian said.

"She's a good dog," Cally said as Sian gulped down more wine.

"I'm sure," Sian said.

"Are you all right?" Cally asked.

"Yeah, why?" Sian slugged back the rest of her wine.

Cally wasn't sure how to say Sian seemed to be drinking a lot of wine. It didn't seem like a wise thing to do when this was the first time they'd seen each other after what happened.

"No reason. I suppose…I wanted to apologise for what happened, and check we're okay," Cally said. She got up to fetch the bottle of wine from the fridge. She decided to put a second pizza in the oven. If Sian was going to drink that heavily, then Cally could try to mitigate it by lining her stomach.

"I already said—don't worry about it. It was a scary situation. I feel bad for ignoring your messages. I was just mad," Sian said.

Cally drank the rest of her wine and refilled both glasses. She put the second frozen pizza in the oven. She was feeling a bit tipsy from drinking her wine so quickly. She was glad she'd put two pizzas in.

"Well, I don't blame you for ignoring me. I'm glad we've made up," Cally said.

"Me too," said Sian, "because now I can get all the gossip about you and Laurie."

Cally groaned. "Is that all round the village as well, then?"

Sian grinned and nodded. "Yep. Since Laurie's late night dash to save the dog."

"Bloody hell," Cally said.

"So go on, dish."

"There's nothing to dish. We get on well and we're having a nice time," Cally said.

Sian snorted. "Yeah, okay. You're having a nice time rattling the headboard together, more like."

Cally felt her face flame, and she shoved Sian gently. "You're so vulgar."

"But also right. If I wasn't with Nick, she might turn me, you know." Sian winked, and Cally wasn't sure if it was what she'd said or the way she said it, but it made Cally uncomfortable. She didn't like it when straight women said stuff like that, anyway.

But Sian was already pretty drunk, and despite what she'd said, there was definitely something going on with her. Cally decided to give her the benefit of the doubt.

"I'd like to meet Nick one day," Cally said.

"I'm not sure you would," Sian said.

Ah, so that was it. Some problem with Nick. Cally didn't think they were good enough friends for her to ask. Maybe Sian would get around to it if she wanted to.

"Sorry. That was a stupid thing to say. Of course you should meet Nick. He asks about you," Sian said. Cally noticed she'd slowed down on the wine a bit.

"Does he?" Cally asked.

"Oh yeah. Wants to know *all* about you," Sian said, and there was a look in her eye, a secretive look Cally didn't much like.

The oven buzzed, and Cally got up to take the food out. "I hope you like frozen pizzas," she said. "It's all I can cook. I'm pretty hopeless in the kitchen," she added, hoping to lighten the mood.

"But I bet you're great in the bedroom."

Cally turned, startled.

"Oh fuck. I'm sorry. I'm *so* sorry, Cally." Sian put her head in her hands and started crying. Cally left the pizzas where they were and went to her.

"Sian, what's going on?" Cally said.

"It's fucking Nick," Sian said without looking up.

"I wondered if it might be," Cally said. "Come on, let's go in the living room. I'll bring the wine and pizza."

"Okay." Sian nodded. "Bring the one I already opened. Sorry about that."

In the living room, Cally started a fire in the wood burner. She sat next to Sian on the sofa. "So, what's happened?"

"You're going to hate me," Sian said.

"No, I won't." Cally poured them both more wine.

"You will, but fuck it." Sian pulled a tissue out of her pocket and blew her nose. "Okay, so when we first got together, he was seeing someone else."

"Right." Cally didn't hate Sian, but after her own experiences with Jules's infidelities, she couldn't help but judge a little.

"I knew it was wrong, but…Well, when you meet him, you'll understand. He's just so…*persuasive*. Anyway, we ended up getting together officially. His marriage broke down, and some other stuff happened."

Cally sipped some of her wine. Sian seemed to have slowed down, which was good. "Okay."

"Anyway, we had a big argument. I found out he still loves his ex.

Even after everything she did to him. He loves her. What would you have done, Cally?"

"What do you mean?" Cally asked.

"If the person you loved most in the world told you they loved someone else," Sian whispered.

Cally felt a shiver run up her spine. The way Sian was looking at her…

"I got rid of him," Sian said, looking away. She picked up her wine glass and fiddled with the stem. "I mean, I kicked him out."

"Oh, Sian. I'm sorry. I'm so sorry. Is he going back to her?" Cally asked and reached out to squeeze Sian's hand.

Sian laughed, and it was bitter. "Oh no. That's the funny part, you see. She met someone else. He is *not* happy, let me tell you."

"I see." Cally didn't really know what to say. She had another drink. She was really hungry but thought it might be a bit insensitive to start eating.

"Do you *see,* Cally?" Sian asked. "Sorry. Sorry. I'm just so *angry.* I gave up everything for him."

"I know how that feels," Cally said.

"I suppose you do. Your wife was famous, wasn't she?" Sian asked.

Cally nodded. "She was. She didn't want me to work. I lost all my friends too."

"But she took care of you, didn't she? Nick never took care of me," Sian said.

"I don't know if I'd call it taking care of me. But I am sorry this happened to you," Cally said.

Something about this conversation was giving Cally a bad feeling. Something about the way Sian was talking didn't feel right. Cally had been looking forward to this evening, and now she wanted Sian to go home. She instantly felt bad. The poor woman's relationship had ended, and all Cally could think about was when Sian would leave and stop creeping her out.

"Yeah, well"—Sian took a small sip of her wine—"some might say it serves me right."

"I don't think that's fair," Cally said. "So, he's gone, then?"

"Oh yeah. He's well and truly gone," Sian said and giggled.

"Well, sounds like you're well shot of him," Cally said, struggling to be empathetic. The whole conversation was making her feel so uncomfortable, and she couldn't understand why.

Sian looked at her, and something in her eyes made Cally lean back and away from her. Then it was gone, and she was just Sian again.

"I've really unloaded on you tonight, haven't I." Sian blew her nose again. "I'm sorry. This was supposed to be a fun night."

"Don't be silly. I'm flattered you trusted me to tell me. It must be horrible for you," Cally said. But she really hoped they could drop the subject now. She was such a horrible person.

"No, he's not going to ruin our girls' night. Come on, let's get some more wine and line our stomachs with this pizza."

Cally smiled and picked up her glass. It looked like tonight was going to be a long one.

CHAPTER FORTY-FOUR

Cally woke with her head pounding. Her mouth felt like the bottom of a hamster cage. She hadn't drunk that much, had she? She looked down and saw she was still fully clothed. Bloody hell. Something pulled at the edges of her memory, a dream maybe. Someone standing over in the night, watching. Cally shivered. It was probably Sian helping her get to bed.

Cally sat up and looked at her phone. The room spun for a second. It was after midday. She never slept that long usually. They must have gone to bed so late. She also saw she hadn't set the house alarm, which was good because there was a text from Sian saying she'd gone home and hoped Cally's head wasn't too bad.

A bath was what she needed, a long soak and then something to eat. Her stomach revolted at the thought of food. Christ, she must have been pissed last night.

Cally shuffled into the bathroom like an old lady and turned the hot tap on the bath. She rummaged in the cupboard for her bubble bath. She saw it near the back and went to reach for it. Her hand stopped in mid air. What the hell? The cupboard didn't look right—or, rather, what was inside it didn't. Her stuff was all there but it looked *different*. Things were moved around. Had she done that last night? Or maybe Sian had. Perhaps when she put Cally to bed, she decided to have a good old rummage in the bathroom. Did people do that? She guessed some must.

The memory of someone standing over her came back into her mind. It must have been a dream because now she remembered.

It was Jules. Jules had been standing over her.

Cally lost the battle with her stomach and vomited into the toilet.

After her bath, a big glass of water, and some dried fruit and nuts, Cally felt better if not completely herself.

She went around the house to see what else might be out of place, and everything looked pretty much as she thought she'd left it. It must have just been Sian having a nose. After the way Sian'd behaved last night, Cally thought that explanation sounded plausible. After last night's conversation, Cally was feeling a bit funny about her. It wasn't that Nick had been married when she'd met him—it was the way she'd told Cally about what was going on for her. It was almost as if Sian was angry at her. Strange.

Cally thought she might leave it awhile before she saw Sian again. There was something about the two of them together that really wasn't gelling—probably just a difference in personality, but Cally also had a suspicion there might be a bit of a mean streak in Sian.

Or maybe she was just hung-over and feeling pissy at everyone.

And speaking of everyone, Laurie hadn't messaged at all. Cally was feeling grumpy about it even though she knew she was being completely unreasonable. Because on one hand, why would Laurie message her? She knew Cally was seeing Sian last night and probably didn't want to interrupt them. But on the other hand, Cally could be lying dead in a ditch and Laurie wouldn't know.

Okay, that was *definitely* unreasonable.

Cally sighed. She was literally sitting here arguing with herself. Laurie didn't owe her anything. Cally had said herself that she wanted things casual, and Laurie was honouring her wishes.

Cally was grumpy because she was hung-over. Although she didn't remember ever feeling this bad before. She felt like she'd been hit by a truck.

It was probably best Laurie hadn't messaged her. She wasn't exactly good company. She hadn't been for a run for ages, either, mainly because of the stalker, but perhaps if she stuck to the busier routes she'd be okay. When she'd been on weekend runs before, she'd seen lots of families and dog walkers out on the trails.

She certainly wasn't in any condition to go running at the moment, though. She'd probably end up passing out and falling in a ditch.

Cally's phone buzzed again. Laurie. With a really nice message that made Cally feel like an arsehole for her earlier dark thoughts.

She wanted to know if Cally was up for a walk in the woods. Cally consulted her stomach. She thought maybe she could manage a walk, and it might be better than a run.

They agreed to meet at Oakhurst Place. It had a car park and a cafe and was the beginning point for a lot of local walks. Cally told Laurie they'd better do a gentle walk due to her hangover. Laurie replied with a laughing emoji.

Chapter Forty-five

The weather stayed nice for their walk. The trails were fairly busy, but Cally didn't mind—safety in numbers. Laurie bought her a coffee from the cafe and pointed out all the different trees and the flowers that were just beginning to push through the ground.

"You'll love it here in the summer," Laurie said as they emerged from one of the more dense parts of the trail.

"I love it here now," Cally said.

"I know, but in summer it completely changes. That's the thing about this place, its beauty keeps changing," Laurie said, and Cally saw her blush. "Sorry, that was a bit over the top."

"No, it's not. You love it here," Cally said. "It's easy to love." *And,* thought Cally, *so are you, I think*. Laurie had a way about her that made Cally feel comfortable and relaxed when she was with her. She needed to be careful—they both did. Or one of them was going to get hurt.

"What's up?" Laurie asked.

"Nothing. What do you mean?" Cally asked.

"You've gone all quiet, and you've got that moody look on your face."

"No, I don't. Do I?"

"Yeah, you do. I've been watching you, and I'm starting to learn when you're thinking about something depressing."

Cally couldn't help laughing. "Fine, maybe I was."

"Why? It's such a nice day. Think about good things instead," Laurie said.

"Is it that simple?" Cally asked, genuinely interested in Laurie's answer.

Laurie shrugged. "It's what I do. Granted, I don't have a stalker, and no one tried to burn my cabins down. But sometimes, you have to just let things go and enjoy the moment."

"You're full of wisdom today," Cally said.

"I meditated this morning, that's why."

"No, you didn't." Cally laughed. "Did you?"

"No." Laurie grinned. "I chopped wood like any self-respecting lesbian would do on a Sunday morning."

Cally laughed. "I don't chop wood. Maybe that's where I've been going wrong."

"Definitely. Now, do you want to go home, or do you want to come back to mine for some lunch and then sex? Or just lunch. Or just sex," Laurie asked.

Cally saw they'd finished their walk and were back at the cafe. "Definitely lunch if it's something light. The sex, I'm going to have to let you know."

"Fair enough," Laurie said.

She took Laurie's hand and led her back to the car park.

It really was easy with Laurie. Cally wished again that she'd met her years ago. Things could have been very different.

In the end, they had a light lunch and then sex. Both were good, and Cally fell asleep in Laurie's bed. When she woke, the curtains were still open and the night was pitch-black outside. Trying not to wake Laurie, Cally carefully climbed out of bed.

She gathered up her clothes, which were scattered around the room, and crept into the hall. When she was dressed, Cally tiptoed to the stairs. She was about to go down when she stopped. Laurie's office was lit up in a warm glow from a desk lamp. Cally glanced towards the bedroom where Laurie slept, then back to the office. She knew she shouldn't go in. She knew it was wrong, but something made her feet move, and instead of going downstairs, she went into the office.

Cally looked around. It looked like any other home office with a desk and a chair. It was neat and tidy like the rest of Laurie's home with everything in its place.

Except for a plastic storage box that sat on the desk.

Cally didn't want to look. She was acutely aware of the massive breach of trust she was about to commit. She just couldn't stop herself. She needed to know. *What* she needed to know she wasn't sure.

Except she was. She *was* sure wasn't she? No point lying to herself.

Cally wanted to know if Laurie was like Jules. As if there would be a gaslighter's manual hidden somewhere in the room, or maybe some other evidence that proved her to be Cally's stalker.

In a couple of steps, Cally reached the box. She looked inside and saw a jumble of assorted belongings, books and DVDs, mostly. She also saw the photo. At least she thought it was the same one Laurie had picked up off the floor and put in her pocket so casually.

Cally's hand shook as she picked it up. It was an image of two women Cally knew intimately. In the photo, Jules had her arm slung around Laurie's shoulders. Both of them were grinning.

Cally dropped the photo back into the box feeling numb. She lifted out one of the DVDs and saw it was one of Jules's old stand-ups. In fact, everything in the box was something to do with Jules.

Jesus fucking Christ. Stuffed down the side and buried beneath several books was something else. Cally pulled it out even though she knew what it was. An orange jacket. Not the one that had been in Laurie's truck, but another one. The one her stalker wore the times she'd seen them.

Cally felt sick. She felt panic rising up inside her. In her head she kept repeating the same thing over and over. *Not Laurie, not Laurie.*

Why did it have to be her?

She had to get out of here. Cally turned to leave. At some point, without her hearing, Laurie had woken up and gotten out of bed. Now she stood blocking the door.

Chapter Forty-six

"What's going on, Cally?" Laurie asked.

She didn't *look* like some crazed stalker. She looked like a woman who'd just woken up and had no idea what Cally'd just found. Her hair was tousled, and her eyes were sleepy.

"I need to leave," Cally whispered.

"Okay. Could you just tell me what happened? And why you're in my office?" Laurie asked, and Cally could see she was becoming more alert.

"I need to *go*," Cally said. She pushed past Laurie and hurried to the landing. Where the fuck were her car keys?

Jacket. They were in her jacket, and she'd hung *that* on the newel post when they came in. Cally ran downstairs and snagged her jacket.

"Cally!" Laurie called. "What the bloody hell is going on?"

Cally didn't answer. She went to the front door, fully expecting it to be locked so she couldn't get out. It wasn't. Just the normal latch. She thumbed it back and ran outside, not bothering to close the door.

Once she was in her car, she smashed the palm of her hand down on the lock button. She glanced up in her rear-view mirror and saw Laurie standing in the doorway looking confused. When Cally started the car, Laurie stayed where she was. She was still standing there as Cally screeched out of her drive.

When she was a decent distance down the road, Cally pulled over. She couldn't stop shaking. She got out her phone and dialled 999 and asked for the police. When she hung up, her phone rang. Laurie. Cally quickly cancelled the call. She drove home and, just like last time, waited in her car for the police to arrive.

They arrived quickly, and when Cally told them what had happened, one of the units left to go to Laurie's house.

The officers who remained took her inside the house. They wanted to call someone to come and be with her, but Cally had no one. She briefly considered Sian, then quickly squashed the idea. She definitely didn't want *her* over. Cally was shocked at how strongly she felt.

In the end, the officers left her alone. She bolted the door, checked all the windows, and set the alarm. Laurie hadn't tried to call again, which meant the police had probably spoken to her.

When Cally told them what she'd found, it didn't seem especially incriminating. The more Cally thought about it, the more she wondered if she hadn't overreacted. Jules had a huge gay following for obvious reasons. It made sense Laurie would have her DVDs and books. It would also make sense she would box them up and put them out of the way where Cally couldn't see.

The orange jacket, though. Why would she have that?

Cally's brain hurt and her heart hurt and she had a headache crashing around behind her eyes. She wanted to go to bed, but she didn't think she'd sleep.

She went into the living room to lie down. She hadn't been in there since the night before, and her and Sian's wine glasses were still on the table. A neat pile of blankets sat on the side. She didn't remember getting them for Sian, but she supposed she must have done, which seemed strange because she had a guest bedroom upstairs. The only reason Sian hadn't slept there last time was because she was too drunk to get up the stairs.

Cally guessed she must have been this time too.

She picked up the wine glasses. The empty bottle Sian had already partially drunk was on the floor.

Cally paused. They must have drunk more than that, surely. Sian had practically a whole bottle to herself in the kitchen. Unless Cally had drunk the majority of this one by herself, there was no way she should have felt as rough as she did.

Cally looked at the glasses. Both empty. She sniffed them, not sure what she thought she might smell. As it was, they just smelled of stale wine. She put them back down. As they touched the coffee table, the lights went out. Cally turned and bumped into the coffee table. She banged her shins and cursed.

Her phone buzzed, and she held it up in the dark to look at the screen. A notification popped up.

Alarm off.

Chapter Forty-seven

Nine months ago

Jules saw the vague shape of her as she walked across the grass. Her irritation grew with every step she took. She was taking her fucking time with it. Jules tried to swallow the anger and bury it. It didn't work. Sometimes she'd managed it for Cally, but never for this fucking idiot.

"What took you so long? I've been here ages," Jules said as soon as she was close enough to hear without Jules having to shout.

"Sorry. I can't always just drop everything."

"Yes, you fucking well can." Jules grabbed her arm and squeezed. "For me you *do*."

"Ouch. You're hurting me." The woman pulled her arm away from Jules.

"You're pathetic. Come on, then, let's walk. We're too close to the road here, and people might see me," Jules said.

The woman rolled her eyes, and Jules's hand itched to slap her face. What had she been thinking, getting mixed up with this moron? She was no Cally.

"Fine. I forgot how famous and important you are."

Jules held her tongue. She didn't want to lose it and have the stupid bitch flounce off now. "Let's walk the path along the edge. We should be out of view there."

The woman hesitated for a moment, and Jules thought she wasn't going to come. Then she huffed and started walking.

"So why all the Secret Squirrel stuff? It's all come out now. We can be together properly." The woman said it in a sulky voice that made Jules wonder again what she'd been thinking of.

"Have you not seen the news? Or read the papers? I'm fucking *wanted*. The police are looking for me. You think we should just trot around Eastbourne arm in arm like young lovers?"

"I didn't say that. I meant let me stand by you while you fight the charges. I don't understand why you're suddenly being so mean."

Jules spun to face her and nearly knocked her off balance. It would have been handy if she'd fallen the other way, to be honest. Straight off the cliff. "Don't you? You're blackmailing me, you idiot."

"I am *not* blackmailing you. I *love* you. I just don't see why you don't hand yourself in and fight your corner in court. I'll be with you the whole way. Your wife is evil, and she needs to be shown up for what she really is."

This woman really was serious. For the love of God. Jules didn't say anything until they reached the spot. She'd gotten here an hour earlier to find the perfect place.

"Cally isn't evil. And there is no way on this *earth* I would have ever picked you over her. You aren't in the same league. You aren't the kind of person someone marries. You're the kind of woman someone fucks a few times and then forgets about. And you must be out of your *mind* if you think I'm going to sail off with you into the sunset and start a new life."

"Why are you being so mean?" She seemed to genuinely want to know.

"Mean? I'm not being mean. I'm being honest. You should have left me alone when I told you to. Following me about like some kind of fucking stalker. You're pathetic. And stupid."

"So stupid I found out where you were hiding."

Jules was bored. She'd had enough of this and had better things to be doing. Once she'd tied up this last loose end, she'd find Cally. And Cally would rue the fucking day she walked out on Jules Kay.

Without warning, Jules reached out for her and pushed.

Chapter Forty-eight

Now

Cally turned on the torch app on her phone. Heart beating fast, she willed herself not to panic. The power had gone, that was all. She thought the alarm was supposed to have some sort of backup system. Her phone buzzed again.

Alarm on. Service interruption restored.

Cally sighed with relief. She went into the hall and checked that the front door was properly locked. Everything looked as it should. She was just jumpy, that was all, and she had good reason to be.

She tried to remember where Laurie had gone that time when the electric went. The fuse box at the top of the basement stairs. She just hoped what she'd need to do would be obvious.

Luckily, it was. A switch had tripped, and Cally was relieved that when she pushed it back up, the lights came on. She was lucky Laurie showed her that, or she would have had no idea what to do.

Cally didn't want to think about Laurie right now. She didn't want to think about what happened earlier tonight, either. Cally *definitely* didn't want to think about whether she'd overreacted. The evidence had been there in the box—the Jules memorabilia, the bloody jacket, for God's sake. The police would likely call her soon to tell her what was happening. They'd say whether they'd arrested Laurie—again.

Arrest her for what, though? Having a box of Jules's DVDs? Cally didn't know much about the law, but she was pretty sure it wasn't an arrestable offence to have those things.

She thought back to when she'd been in Laurie's office. Laurie hadn't tried to stop her from leaving. She could have easily overpowered Cally if she wanted. Had Cally made a terrible mistake? If she had, then surely there was no way Laurie would forgive her again so easily.

Cally went into the living room and pulled the blankets around her. She lay down on the sofa and tried not to think about whether she'd made a horrible error and probably lost Laurie for good.

At some point, she must have fallen asleep because she woke to the sound of her phone ringing. She checked caller ID and saw it was the detective in charge of her case. Cally answered it before the detective rang off.

She listened as the officer told her they'd searched Laurie's house with her permission and found nothing. She said she understood when the detective explained they couldn't arrest Laurie for having a box of Jules Kay merchandise in her office. She said she was sorry and that they were still following up leads. She said she'd advised Laurie not to contact Cally.

Cally hung up the phone, leaned back on the sofa, and cried. What the fuck had she done? The detective had been kind and understanding, but Cally thought she'd probably pegged Cally for a nutjob by now, as someone who had a vendetta against Laurie and was paranoid to the extreme. The detective was probably beginning to question if anyone was even stalking Cally at all. Not that she'd said that or even hinted it. Of course she hadn't, she'd been nothing but professional and would probably do her job whatever her personal beliefs.

Cally felt like a nutter and was probably projecting. Laurie had been told not to contact her, but that didn't mean she couldn't contact Laurie, did it?

Before she could consider what she was doing, Cally dialled her number. She didn't expect Laurie to pick up, and the phone rang for a long time.

"I nearly didn't pick up." Laurie sounded tired but awake. Cally hadn't woken her.

"I don't blame you. I probably wouldn't have in your situation," Cally said.

"What do you want?" Laurie's voice was cold, and Cally didn't blame her for that, either.

"To say I'm sorry."

"What for? For running out of my house in the middle of the night with no explanation? Or for sending the police to my door?"

"Both. All of it," Cally said. She was so tired.

"Well, you've said sorry, so I'm going to hang up now," Laurie said.

"Laurie, please. Don't," Cally said, and to her mortification, she started to cry. "I'm sorry. I'm so sorry."

Laurie sighed. "Cally. Look, I get you're scared. I understand that. And I really didn't blame you for the first time when you thought it was me. But I thought we'd moved on, you know, got close. You met my *family*, for fuck's sake."

"I know."

"Why are you so sure I'm the one stalking you?" Laurie asked.

"I'm not. Not at all. I saw the box and panicked," Cally said.

"If you'd let me explain, I would have told you. The stuff, the photo, I had it around the house. When we started hanging out, I put it away. I'd meant to do it before I even met you because of what she did. I took the photo out of its frame, but then I just stuffed it behind another picture," Laurie said.

It all made complete and perfect sense. All except one thing. "What about the jacket?"

Laurie remained silent for a moment. "Oh, that."

Cally's heart thudded in her chest. The silence between them was thick and heavy. Cally waited for the answer.

"I can't explain it," Laurie said. "I told the police it wasn't mine. I don't know how it got there, Cally. I'm aware that's probably going to make you think it's me even more than you already do."

Except it did the opposite. If it was Laurie, wouldn't she have just lied? "I don't understand. How did it get there if it's not yours?" Cally asked.

"I don't know. You're the only person who's been in my house lately," Laurie said.

"Well, it wasn't me," Cally said.

"Are you sure?" Laurie asked.

Cally was angry. "Yes, I'm bloody sure. How dare you."

"Not nice, is it? Being accused," Laurie said.

Cally didn't have an answer for that. "Fine. You've made your point."

"I don't think I have. I've been *arrested* because of you. And now, police show up at my door and search *all* through my house, and I feel like a criminal because of *you*," Laurie said.

"Wait a minute," Cally said.

"No, I will not. I—"

"Laurie. The day I came over to your house. The day we…you know."

"Yes, I know." Laurie sounded weary.

"I thought there was someone in your house. Remember? I thought I saw someone upstairs," Cally said. Her brain was ticking and whirring and piecing things together, and she wondered again if she was going nuts.

"Yeah, you thought I had a girlfriend or something," Laurie said.

"What if I *did* see someone in your house?" Cally asked.

"You didn't. There wasn't anyone in there. I live alone," Laurie said.

"I know, but what if someone got in? What if *they* put the jacket in the box? Was the box there by then?" Cally asked.

"Yeah, it was. I put it up there after the first time you came over. I was hoping you'd come again," Laurie said. "But my house wasn't broken into."

"You left the door unlocked—or it was unlocked *by* someone. Do you remember if you locked it when you went out?" Cally asked.

Laurie was quiet for a moment. "I don't know. I lock it if I remember and leave it if I don't. It's the country."

"So someone could have got in," Cally said.

"Got in and put a jacket in my office? Why?" Laurie asked.

"So I would think it was you stalking me," Cally said.

"Cally, that's really far-fetched. It relies on them knowing you would go in there and find it. What if I found it first and threw it out?" Laurie asked.

"Well…I mean, I suppose that's possible," Cally said. That had thrown her. What Laurie said was true. And it was far-fetched, wasn't it? This whole thing was far-fetched.

"Look, Cally," Laurie said, and Cally braced herself for what was coming next. "I'm sorry for you, for your situation. I can't imagine what it's like to have someone stalk you. But—"

"I know what you're going to say," Cally said.

"I just don't think we should see each other any more. I can't keep being suspected and being arrested and having my house turned over by the police."

"I understand," Cally said and willed herself not to cry.

"I'm sorry," Laurie said, and the line went dead.

Cally couldn't blame her. Everything she said was true. Cally was surprised she'd lasted this long, frankly. She wasn't sure she'd have been so forgiving if Laurie had her arrested.

And part of Cally—a very small part—thought it was probably for the best. It could still be Laurie. Mostly, Cally didn't think it was any more, but who knew?

She didn't trust anyone, not even herself now.

She was isolated and alone and scared and unsure. All the things the stalker probably wanted. They'd won. Congratulations, them.

Cally pulled the blankets around herself and lay back down to sleep.

Chapter Forty-nine

When Cally came downstairs, she almost absently picked up the letter off the doormat. Robotically, she opened it, making sure to hold it by the corners and read the latest number: 0. She sighed, put the letter back in the envelope, and put it to one side for the police.

Martha—that's what she decided to call the dog—came trotting out of the living room to greet her good morning. The first couple of days had been tricky. Martha hid under the kitchen table and refused to come out. Cally was instructed not to let her outside yet because her feet were still sore. When she *did* eventually let her out, she'd have to keep her on a lead for a while, in case she ran off.

They'd become what Cally would describe as acquaintances, bordering on friends.

Which was a good thing because Cally certainly had none of *them* left in the human world.

She'd not heard from Laurie since that night, and she'd avoided Sian's messages. She'd replied to the last one because she didn't want to appear too rude, but she'd been evasive about meeting up.

Cally had basically become a hermit. If not for the workmen in and out of Five Oaks all day, she'd have seen no one at all. And now she had plenty of time to think about what the numbers meant, not that it took a rocket scientist. Apparently, she was out of time. Whatever the stalker had planned was likely imminent.

The police had posted a car outside her house for the last couple of days, ever since the numbers got lower. They sat at the bottom of her drive, and Cally brought them tea and coffee and sometimes sandwiches. They were there for her benefit, but she felt like a prisoner.

The dog chuffed lightly, and Cally realised she'd been standing in her hall for almost four minutes. "Sorry, girl," she said. "Let's get your breakfast."

Cally suspected food was the thing helping her bond with the dog fastest. Martha was bloody greedy, and it was sausages that got her to finally come out from under the table. Cally didn't think she'd make sausages a regular thing, but while she was trying to get Martha to put on weight, it didn't seem to matter.

She went into the kitchen and gave Martha her breakfast. She sat down at the kitchen table and contemplated the long, empty day ahead of her. She tried to remember if there was any paperwork she needed to do. God, things must be dire if she was hoping she had to do paperwork.

Cally's phone buzzed, and she briefly wondered—hoped—it might be Laurie. Of course, it wouldn't be. And Cally wished she could just let it go.

She looked at the icon on the screen and sucked in a breath.

Alarm off.

Maybe the workmen had put a pickaxe through a line. Martha padded gently to the kitchen door and growled low in her throat. She stared down the hall at something Cally couldn't see.

Then, one by one, the locks on the front door clicked and the door opened. Cally stood up. She was strangely calm. She supposed she had been waiting for this for a while now.

Sian stepped through the doorway. She closed the door gently behind her.

"Call that mutt away, or I'll hurt her," she said in the same friendly tone she always used to speak to Cally.

Cally called Martha. Martha looked from Cally to Sian and back again. She gave a low bark then came over.

"Shut her in the utility room," Sian instructed. "Good. Now, we have some things to talk about."

Cally backed up until she hit the worktop behind her. "What are you doing here, Sian?" Except she knew. Of course she knew.

"I gave you a countdown," Sian said. "You knew today was the day."

"How did you get past the police?" Cally asked, stalling for time.

"Oh, I didn't come that way. I walked through the forest from

Laurie's house. Your workmen just waved at me. I've made sure they've seen me here before."

Cally's heart started to thump in her chest at the mention of Laurie. "What did you do to her?"

Sian smiled and waved her hand. "Oh, don't worry about *her*. You've got much bigger problems."

In the utility room, Martha scratched at the door and whined. "She doesn't like being shut in."

"I bet. I tried to be her friend when she lived in your cabin. She wouldn't come near me, though. Funny, that," Sian said.

"You know, I thought your entrance would be much more dramatic," Cally said.

"What do you mean?"

"I thought you'd turn off the electric again. I thought you'd come at night," Cally said.

Sian laughed. "That would have been better. But I have things to do and not much time. You're coming with me, don't worry. I need you to take these pills for me."

Cally knew that no matter what happened, she wasn't taking any pill. "Where are we going?"

"It's a surprise. Now, I'm sure you know by now that Laurie isn't in a good way. I haven't killed her, but she definitely needs a hospital. If you take the pills, I'll call an ambulance for her. If you don't, I'll let her bleed out."

Cally felt the world recede and she had to hold on to the worktop to keep upright. "What the fuck is *wrong* with you?"

"We'll get to that. I mean, mostly I just fucking hate you. You know how difficult it's been, pretending to be your friend? Do you know how much wine I had to drink just to get through an evening with you?" Sian rolled her eyes. "Take the pills."

"No. You won't call an ambulance for Laurie. I know you won't," Cally said.

"And you'll be able to live with yourself knowing you made the decision she should die?" Sian asked.

"Not my decision. I won't feel guilty for what you've done," Cally said.

"Of course you won't. You never do," Sian said.

"What does that *mean*? I don't even *know* you," Cally said.

"No, you don't, but I know you. I know *all* about you. Jules couldn't stop fucking talking about you," Sian said.

"Jules? You knew Jules."

Cally had the horrible feeling that Jules would walk into the room any moment for the big reveal.

"Oh, don't worry. She's dead. I killed her. It was an accident on my part and I blame you."

And there it was. It all came back to bloody Jules. She might be dead—if Sian was to be believed—but she was still making Cally's life a misery. Would it ever end? Cally guessed it might, today, if Sian had her way.

"I'm not going to ask you again. Take the pills," Sian said.

"Go fuck yourself," said Cally.

CHAPTER FIFTY

Nine months ago

Sian had come here to talk to Jules. She was trying to help her. When they'd met, Jules had been all charm and interest. Slowly, though, over the months they'd been seeing each other, things had changed. Until one day when Jules called it quits. She hadn't even had the decency to do it in person. She'd sent a text.

Jules hadn't known who she was dealing with, though. She was used to that insipid little church mouse of a wife, a nodding dog who did what she was told. Sian wouldn't go quietly. She had to make Jules see what a mistake she'd made. So, she messaged her and turned up at her work from time to time.

The last time, Jules threatened her. Told her to stay away, and when Sian—only out of anger—told Jules she was going to tell Cally what they'd been doing, Jules actually hit her.

Sian couldn't believe it. She'd never been hit by anyone in her life, and here was Jules, laying her out cold.

Sian forgave her, though. It was Cally who was making her like this. Cally who had Jules under her thumb. Who embarrassed her on purpose and treated her badly. Jules said it herself.

So, it didn't make sense when Jules ended it over text, saying she owed it to her marriage to try to make things work. That was it. One text, see you later, thanks for applying but we went with another candidate. Then Jules blocked her, and that's when Sian knew this was Cally's doing.

Cally must have found out about them somehow, and she had something, some secret that she used to keep Jules in that loveless marriage. Sian decided she needed to help Jules. She needed to come up with a plan that would allow Jules to get out of the nightmare she was living in.

Then the whole thing with the knife happened. Cally again. Sian knew she made it all up. She just *knew* Jules would never have gone after anyone with a knife, and definitely not Cally.

And then, a miracle. Jules contacted her just like she knew she would, once she was free of that weight around her neck.

She apologised for the way she'd behaved and told Sian she was scared of Cally. That *finally* Cally had done the thing she'd been blackmailing Jules with. Jules cried and Sian held her and then they made love, and Jules told her she loved her. It was all Sian ever wanted, and she didn't think she'd ever been that happy.

Then the accident happened.

Whenever Sian thought about it, she could barely breathe. The greatest love of her life gone, just like that. And the things she said. Terrible things. But she hadn't meant them. She'd been scared. Cally still had a hold over her—that was proven when Jules said the things she had.

When Jules fell over the side of that cliff, Sian screamed. She couldn't stop screaming. She was surprised no one came, but then she was shouting into the wind. That was when Sian decided she had to make Cally pay for her crime—she might as well have murdered Jules herself. Sian was going to make *her* suffer, make her wish she was dead. Then she would kill her.

By the time she was finished, Cally would probably thank her.

Chapter Fifty-one

Now

Cally waited for Sian's next move. The one thing she was sure of was that she would fight Sian before she took any pills. And Cally thought she probably stood a good chance against her. She couldn't think about Laurie lying bleeding somewhere. Getting away from Sian was the best chance Laurie had of surviving, not taking her fucking pill.

Martha was starting to whine at the utility room door. Sian didn't seem to hear.

"Are you going to take the pill or not?" Sian asked.

"Not," Cally replied and was surprised at how strong her voice sounded.

"Jules said you were stubborn," Sian said.

Cally snorted. "Stubborn? Not with her I wasn't. She bulldozed and bullied her way over anything I wanted. But you probably know that."

"How dare you speak about her like that. She was worth ten of you," Sian said. "Last chance to take the pill."

Cally sat and waited.

"Fine." Sian looked almost regretful. She reached under her coat behind her back. "We'll do it the less fun way."

It took Cally half a second to realise Sian had a gun. It took her another half a second to dive out of the chair.

The boom of the shotgun was deafening in the kitchen. Martha began to howl and batter herself against the utility room door.

Cally rolled away from the table and came up in a crouch. Surely the workmen heard that? Surely *someone* heard that?

"We're in the country—no one will bat an eye." Sian pulled the trigger again, and the table splintered. Wood flew everywhere. Cally felt like she was in a fucking Western movie. Sian had fired two shots, though. Didn't shotguns only have two bullets? Except what Cally saw hadn't looked exactly like a shotgun—it was much shorter.

She guessed she was going to have to find out. Sian had gone quiet, and Cally didn't dare poke her head up from behind the kitchen chair she was hiding against. Martha continued to throw herself against the door, and Cally could see it was starting to split. The last thing she wanted was the dog taking a bullet.

Cally decided to take a chance. She poked her head up quickly, expecting to have it blown off or a gun pointed in her face. Neither happened.

Sian was gone—out of the kitchen, at least. Cally looked for her phone. Gone. Sian must have taken it.

She tiptoed to the kitchen door and listened. Silence. Did she dare step into the hall and risk being ambushed by Sian, who was definitely in the house somewhere, still?

What else was she going to do? Sian had turned the deadbolt on the door when she came in, and Cally didn't have the key to unlock it. She would have to get to one of the large windows in the living room and climb out. She considered the one in the kitchen briefly, but it didn't open wide enough. If she broke it, she risked making too much noise and alerting Sian to where she was.

Cally looked out into the hallway again. There were three doors off it, so three places Sian could be hiding—behind the basement door, the bathroom door, or the living room door. She was just as likely to have gone upstairs.

Cally made a decision. She bolted down the hall, staying low, and flattened herself against the wall by the living room like some TV show cop.

She waited. She listened.

She couldn't hear Sian in there. Cally looked around the door quickly and saw the room was empty. She could feel the relief wash through her.

Cally ran to the window in some horrible déjà vu of nine months ago and unlocked the window as quietly as she could. She pushed up the window frame.

Behind her came a loud crack, then crashing, panting, and the most vicious barking Cally ever heard.

Martha.

Cally ran to the door just as Martha ran past her without a second glance. She tore up the stairs like a bat out of hell.

"Martha, no!" Cally screamed. Sian would kill her—Cally knew it.

Without much thought, Cally charged up the stairs after her.

CHAPTER FIFTY-TWO

Nine months ago

Jules reached out to push her, and suddenly, she was gone. Jules couldn't control the momentum of her body, and she fell forward right on the edge. In the dark, she could just about make out the sea smashing against the rocks below her and felt it was somehow inevitable that she would go over.

On the heels of that came total shock.

She was Jules Kay. She was going to live forever.

Just as it seemed she would go over, Jules managed catch herself—all those yoga and Pilates classes not wasted—and stopped her inevitable fall. Gravel skittered under her feet and bounced off the rocks below. Relief surged through her as she pinwheeled her arms to keep her balance. She'd done it, prevented total disaster.

It was the push against her back that did it. Hard and deliberate, Jules felt hands shove against her. She didn't stand a chance. She lost her battle with gravity and went over the edge. She tumbled over and over, hitting the rocks with a *thud, thud, thud* as she bounced her way down. She splashed into the sea, and by now she could feel nothing. She let the waves take her under.

Above her, she could see the vague shape of a woman watching her. Then she was gone.

❖

Sian watched Jules disappear beneath the sea. She had her phone torch out and tried to follow her progress. Sian thought Jules surfaced one more time before she went under forever.

At the moment, she was numb. She thought the grief would follow. What a terrible, terrible tragedy. Sian replayed events in her mind. Jules must have thought Sian was about to fall over the edge, and like the hero she was, she reached out to save her. Tragically, she ended up going over the side herself.

Sian allowed the tears to come. It was just so awful. Jules died trying to save *her*. If the newspapers knew *that* information, they wouldn't be printing so many horrible lies.

Sian knew what she had to do next. Cally was the reason for all of this. First, she'd stood in the way of Sian and Jules and their love. Now she'd killed her. Not *literally*, but they wouldn't even have been up here if it wasn't for that duplicitous cunt.

Sian left the cliff and went back to her hotel. She checked out early the next morning and went back to London. Then she waited and watched.

Cally—the dumb bitch—had no idea Sian had eyes on her. She watched her every day, all day. She lost her job. Luckily, her pathetic, senile parents lent her money. She gave up the tenancy on her flat. She wouldn't need it anyway because she practically lived in her car those first couple of months.

When she found out Cally bought Five Oaks—she'd followed her on the Tube one day and been privy to a long and boring conversation between Cally and her business manager—she went up straight away. She thought it would put her above suspicion if she already lived there by the time Cally showed up.

Sian borrowed more money off her idiot parents to open the bakery. They had to re-mortgage their house. Sian didn't understand why they were so worried about it—it would be her house when they finally popped their useless old clogs.

So, she went up there to that nothing little village and waited. It only took a couple of months for Cally to show up. And the rest was history.

Chapter Fifty-three

Now

Cally heard Sian scream, and another gunshot went off. Cally raced along the landing and, without thinking of the risks, charged straight into her bedroom.

Sian was there, standing on her bed. She still held the gun out in front of her. Martha lay on the carpet, and she was still.

"No," Cally whispered. "No, no, no." She looked up at Sian, who seemed just as shocked.

"That was your fault," Sian said. "I didn't want to hurt it. That's why I told you to shut it away. Now look what you've done. Another death you're responsible for."

"No," Cally said.

"*Yes*. Now, there's one more cartridge in this gun. Unless you want it in you, turn around and walk back downstairs. *Now.*" Sian aimed the gun at Cally.

Defeated, Cally did what she was told. What else could she do? Sian had shot the dog that she didn't have any problem with. Cally was sure she would shoot her with a lot less remorse.

Cally walked back out onto the landing with Sian following behind. "Why are you doing this? I don't even know you."

"For Jules," Sian said. "Downstairs."

Cally started to go down. "I thought we were friends."

"Friends?" Sian asked. "*Friends*? I can't fucking stand you. It used to make my skin crawl, sucking up to you and being all pally-pally. You're pathetic."

Cally heard the distant wail of a siren. It was getting closer. Sian must have heard it too.

"Shit," Sian said. "Okay, back up the stairs."

Cally hesitated.

"*Now.* I swear to God, Cally, I'll happily shoot a hole in your little blond head."

Cally knew she would. She backed up the stairs slowly. Sian was walking backwards, keeping her distance.

"Stop. The cord to the attic above your head. Pull it. Pull the ladder down." Sian gestured to the ceiling with the barrel of the gun. How did Sian know that was there?

"*Now.*"

Cally did as she was told. The ladder came down smoothly.

"Up." Sian indicated with the gun again. "And if you fuck about, I will shoot you."

Cally climbed up the ladder obediently and into the attic. She stepped back to wait for Sian.

She realised this was her best opportunity. If Sian was taking her up to the attic and effectively trapping them in the house, then she had no intention of letting Cally live. She'd kill her up here among the dust and the junk.

Cally looked around quickly. Despite her current circumstances, she still felt sick. There had never been any squirrels up here. That's why the pest control man couldn't find any. It had been Sian all along. There was a sleeping bag in one corner with a small pile of clothes and a book next to them. Jesus. Cally guessed she must have hidden them when the pest control man came.

Sian's head popped up above the attic hatch. The barrel of the gun came up almost as quickly, and Cally knew she'd probably get shot if she tried to kick Sian down the ladder.

The sirens were even louder now, and Cally thought they must be coming up the drive.

"Now what?" Cally asked.

Sian stood by the hatch with the gun trained on her. "Now, I fucking kill you."

"They'll catch you," Cally said.

Sian laughed. "You think I care about that? All I want is justice.

Also," Sian said, checking her watch, "your little fuck buddy is probably dead by now. Nice going."

Cally couldn't think about that. She had to think of a way out of this. She looked around the attic but could see nothing.

"Any last words?" Sian asked and smiled. "I saw that in a film once, and I always wanted to say it."

Cally didn't have any. She wanted to tell Laurie and Martha she was sorry. She guessed it didn't matter now—she'd be joining them soon anyway. Then she saw something. She wasn't sure she'd seen what she thought she'd seen, couldn't acknowledge it, since she was probably wrong. Nevertheless hope surged in her.

"Actually, yeah. Go fuck yourself, you nutjob," Cally said and ducked.

But now she was *certain* of what she'd seen.

A hand came up through the attic hatch and grabbed Sian's ankle and pulled.

Sian fell backwards, the gun went off, and Cally prayed it hadn't got her. Sian disappeared down the hatch.

Cally ran to the ladder. She could see Sian lying on the floor next to—

Oh God, it was *Laurie*.

Cally climbed down the ladder. Laurie rolled away from Sian and sat up. Cally could see immediately she was hurt. There was blood across her shirt, and she was so very pale.

"Laurie—"

"I'm okay. We need to hold her down. I think she knocked herself out, but she's a fucking cockroach. She'll bounce back quick."

Cally wasn't so sure. There was a lot of blood where her head lay. All the same, she rolled Sian onto her front and pulled her hands behind her back. Cally reminded herself again of some second rate TV show copper.

Laurie leaned against the banister, tipped her head back, and closed her eyes. Downstairs, Cally could hear the sound of police bludgeoning her door, trying to get in.

"Stay with me, Laurie," she said. "They're almost here."

Laurie gave her a faint smile. "I'm fine. Just resting my eyes."

"Sure you are," Cally said, glad that Laurie could still make a joke.

"We're even now," Laurie said.

"What do you mean?"

"You saved my life. Now I saved yours. Even-steven," Laurie said.

Downstairs, the police finally battered through the door.

"Up here," Cally shouted. "We're up here. Laurie's injured."

"It's not that bad," Laurie said.

Cally rolled her eyes. "And we aren't even. I dragged you across the lake. All you did was give nutso here an ankle tap."

Laurie smiled weakly again. "I dispute your version of events."

Cally could hear heavy booted feet running up the stairs. She closed her eyes too. It was finally over.

Epilogue

One year later

Laurie was moaning about the pain in her shoulder again. Cally noticed how it always seemed to coincide with a task she didn't want to do.

"The people in that cabin are bloody evil. I'm telling you, Cally. Don't make me go down *again* to see what they want," Laurie whined.

Cally rolled her eyes. "I went last time, so this time it's your go."

"But my shoulder," Laurie said.

"Pregnancy trumps a bad shoulder. Get a move on before they complain again," Cally said. She rubbed her back and waddled over to the sink. The baby was due any day now, and as far as she was concerned, it couldn't come soon enough.

"Fine. You can't use that excuse forever, though," Laurie said and walked over. She kissed Cally softly on the mouth and patted the bump.

"Watch me," Cally replied and laughed when Laurie swatted her bum.

Martha chose that moment to limp into the kitchen and stare at Cally. Laurie was convinced that when she did that, she was trying to psychically transmit she wanted cheese. Cally wasn't so sure. Mostly, though, they gave it to her.

After Sian shot her, it had been touch-and-go. Cally had been certain she was dead. It was one of the officers who carried Martha outside in his arms.

She was busy arguing with Laurie—who didn't want to be loaded into the ambulance because apparently Cally could just give her a lift to the hospital—when she saw Martha being brought out, just about still alive.

She'd done a deal with Laurie then. Laurie went into the ambulance, and Cally drove Martha to the vet.

In the end, though, the officer—a big dog lover—drove them there on blue lights.

Martha looked at Cally now as if to say *I helped save your life. Give me a snack.*

"Give her a snack, then," Laurie said.

"Laurie, she can't just eat whatever she wants. It's bad for her," Cally said. "Also, weren't you going down to the cabins?"

Laurie sighed. "Yeah." She walked over to Cally and pulled her into her arms. She kissed her gently on the tip of her nose. "Love you."

"Love you too," Cally said. And she meant it.

A year ago she'd never imagined she would have this. A relationship where she was loved and respected. Laurie was patient and kind and everything Cally could want. The business was going well, and they were fully booked for the summer already.

Cally touched her bump and smiled. These days, the only eyes that watched her were Laurie's loving ones. And of course, Martha's hungry ones, always hustling for cheese.

Cally gave in. "Fine, just one small square," she said and laughed as Martha seemed to understand and danced around her.

About the Author

Eden Darry now lives in Kent, having previously been a lifelong Londoner. She lives with her wife, a dog, and two cats and has four novels published with Bold Strokes Books: *The House*, *Vanished*, *Z-Town*, and *Quiet Village*.

Books Available From Bold Strokes Books

Appalachian Awakening by Nance Sparks. The more Amber's and Leslie's paths cross, the more this hike of a lifetime begins to look like a love of a lifetime. (978-1-63679-527-0)

Dreamer by Kris Bryant. When life seems to be too good to be true and love is within reach, Sawyer and Macey discover the truth about the town of Ladybug Junction, and the cold light of reality tests the hearts of these dreamers. (978-1-63679-378-8)

Eyes on Her by Eden Darry. When increasingly violent acts of sabotage threaten to derail the opening of her glamping business, Callie Pope is sure her ex, Jules, has something to do with it. But Jules is dead…isn't she? (978-1-63679-214-9)

Letters from Sarah by Joy Argento. A simple mistake brought them together, but Sarah must release past love to create a future with Lindsey she never dreamed possible. (978-1-63679-509-6)

Lost in the Wild by Kadyan. When their plane crash-lands, Allison and Mike face hunger, cold, a terrifying encounter with a bear, and feelings for each other neither expects. (978-1-63679-545-4)

Not Just Friends by Jordan Meadows. A tragedy leaves Jen struggling to figure out who she is and what is important to her. (978-1-63679-517-1)

Of Auras and Shadows by Jennifer Karter. Eryn and Rina's unexpected love may be exactly what the Community needs to heal the rot that comes not from the fetid Dark Lands that surround the Community but from within. (978-1-63679-541-6)

The Secret Duchess by Jane Walsh. A determined widow defies a duke and falls in love with a fashionable spinster in a fight for her rightful home. (978-1-63679-519-5)

Winter's Spell by Ursula Klein. When former college roommates reunite at a wedding in Provincetown, sparks fly, but can they find true love when evil sirens and trickster mermaids get in the way? (978-1-63679-503-4)

Coasting and Crashing by Ana Hartnett. Life comes easy to Emma Wilson until Lake Palmer shows up at Alder University and derails her every plan. (978-1-63679-511-9)

Every Beat of Her Heart by KC Richardson. Piper and Gillian have their own fears about falling in love, but will they be able to overcome those feelings once they learn each other's secrets? (978-1-63679-515-7)

Fire in the Sky by Radclyffe and Julie Cannon. Two women from different worlds have nothing in common and every reason to wish they'd never met—except for the attraction neither can deny. (978-1-63679-561-4)

Grave Consequences by Sandra Barret. A decade after necromancy became licensed and legalized, can Tamar and Maddy overcome the lingering prejudice against their kind and their growing attraction to each other to uncover a plot that threatens both their lives? (978-1-63679-467-9)

Haunted by Myth by Barbara Ann Wright. When ghost-hunter Chloe seeks an answer to the current spectral epidemic, all clues point to one very famous face: Helen of Troy, whose motives are more complicated than history suggests and whose charms few can resist. (978-1-63679-461-7)

Invisible by Anna Larner. When medical school dropout Phoebe Frink falls for the shy costume shop assistant Violet Unwin, everything about their love feels certain, but can the same be said about their future? (978-1-63679-469-3)

Like They Do in the Movies by Nan Campbell. Celebrity gossip writer Fran Underhill becomes Chelsea Cartwright's personal assistant with the aim of taking the popular actress down, but neither of them anticipates the clash of their attraction. (978-1-63679-525-6)

Limelight by Gun Brooke. Liberty Bell and Palmer Elliston loathe each other. They clash every week on the hottest new TV show, until Liberty starts to sing and the impossible happens. (978-1-63679-192-0)

Playing with Matches by Georgia Beers. To help save Cori's store and help Liz survive her ex's wedding, they strike a deal: a fake relationship, but just for one week. There's no way this will turn into the real deal. (978-1-63679-507-2)

The Memories of Marlie Rose by Morgan Lee Miller. Broadway legend Marlie Rose undergoes a procedure to erase all of her unwanted memories, but as she starts regretting her decision, she discovers that the only person who could help is the love she's trying to forget. (978-1-63679-347-4)

The Murders at Sugar Mill Farm by Ronica Black. A serial killer is on the loose in southern Louisiana, and it's up to three women to solve the case while carefully dancing around feelings for each other. (978-1-63679-455-6)

A Talent Ignited by Suzanne Lenoir. When Evelyne is abducted and Annika believes she has been abandoned, they must risk everything to find each other again. (978-1-63679-483-9)

All Things Beautiful by Alaina Erdell. Casey Norford only planned to learn to paint like her mentor, Leighton Vaughn, not sleep with her. (978-1-63679-479-2)

An Atlas to Forever by Krystina Rivers. Can Atlas, a difficult dog Ellie inherits after the death of her best friend, help the busy hopeless romantic find forever love with commitment-phobic animal behaviorist Hayden Brandt? (978-1-63679-451-8)

Bait and Witch by Clifford Mae Henderson. When Zeddi gets an unexpected inheritance from her client Mags, she discovers that Mags served as high priestess to a dwindling coven of old witches—who are positive that Mags was murdered. Zeddi owes it to her to uncover the truth. (978-1-63679-535-5)

Buried Secrets by Sheri Lewis Wohl. Tuesday and Addie, along with Tuesday's dog, Tripper, struggle to solve a twenty-five-year-old mystery while searching for love and redemption along the way. (978-1-63679-396-2)

Come Find Me in the Midnight Sun by Bailey Bridgewater. In Alaska, disappearing is the easy part. When two men go missing, state trooper Louisa Linebach must solve the case, and when she thinks she's coming close, she's wrong. (978-1-63679-566-9)

Death on the Water by CJ Birch. The *Ocean Summit*'s authorities have ruled a death on board its inaugural cruise as a suicide, but Claire suspects murder, and with the help of Assistant Cruise Director Moira, Claire conducts her own investigation. (978-1-63679-497-6)

Living For You by Jenny Frame. Can Sera Debrek face real and personal demons to help save the world from darkness and open her heart to love? (978-1-63679-491-4)

Ride with Me by Jenna Jarvis. When Lucy's vacation to find herself becomes Emma's chance to remember herself, they realize that everything they're looking for might already be sitting right next to them—if they're willing to reach for it. (978-1-63679-499-0)

Rivals for Love by Ali Vali. Brooks Boseman's brother Curtis is getting married, and Brooks needs to be at the engagement party. Only she can't possibly go, not with Curtis set to marry the secret love of her youth, Fallon Goodwin. (978-1-63679-384-9)

Whiskey and Wine by Kelly and Tana Fireside. Winemaker Tessa Williams and sex toy shop owner Lace Reynolds are both used to taking risks, but will they be willing to put their friendship on the line if it gives them a shot at finding forever love? (978-1-63679-531-7)

Hands of the Morri by Heather K O'Malley. Discovering she is a Lost Sister and growing acquainted with her new body, Asche learns how to be a warrior and commune with the Goddess the Hands serve, the Morri. (978-1-63679-465-5)

I Know About You by Erin Kaste. With her stalker inching closer to the truth, Cary Smith is forced to face the past she's tried desperately to forget. (978-1-63679-513-3)

Mate of Her Own by Elena Abbott. When Heather McKenna finally confronts the family who cursed her, her werewolf is shocked to discover her one true mate, and that's only the beginning. (978-1-63679-481-5)

Pumpkin Spice by Tagan Shepard. For Nicki, new love is making this pumpkin spice season sweeter than expected. (978-1-63679-388-7)